A PLACE CALLED HOME

SOPHIE HAYDON

BAY BOOKS

A Place Called Home
by Sophie Haydon

An art restorer looking for a home. A man struggling to cope after the death of his wife. And a painting which brings them together but which reveals a mysterious past from which neither can escape...

—The Mackenzies—
A Place Called Home
Secrets at Parata Bay
Escape to Shelter Springs
What you See in the Stars
Second Chance at Whisper Creek
Summer at the Lakehouse Café

—Lantern Bay—
Yours to Give
Yours to Treasure
Yours to Cherish
Yours to Keep
Yours Forever
Yours to Love

https://sophiehaydon.com

© 2017 Diana Fraser
ISBN 978-0-9951447-0-5 (epub)
ISBN 978-1-99-102105-2 (Print - Amazon)
ISBN 978-1-99-102124-3 (Print - Draft2Digital)

CONTENTS

CHAPTER ONE

Lucia scanned the museum's function room—from the elaborate contemporary Maori carvings to the impressive stained-glass wall in all shades and hues of the sky—but she couldn't find who she was looking for. Then she looked at the stage where a TV crew was preparing for the cookery demonstration, and she saw him.

Standing with his back to her, mingling with Wellington's wealthiest and most influential citizens, was her ex-boyfriend.

She nudged her best friend, Rachel, who was waiting for her TV crew to finish their preparations, before taking the stage. "You see, right there, *that* is what I'm talking about." She sighed and sipped her champagne.

Rachel followed Lucia's gaze to Dallas Mackenzie, who was enjoying the company of not one, but two glamorous women. "So?"

"We only stopped dating a few weeks ago, and he's already moved on!"

"And so should you," commented Rachel, as she nodded to the TV crew who were readying themselves to record her regular cookery show, live in front of a high-paying audience. "Look, Lu, forget him."

"Oh, I have. It's just..." Lucia shook her head, as she tried to put into words her frustration at not finding the right man. "It's just *disappointing*, I guess."

"Doesn't sound like it was love, then."

"No. Just as well. But he's a nice man. A good man."

"Just not the man for you."

"Apparently not."

"Then stop watching him and go mingle. Dallas is the only man you've dated since you arrived in New Zealand. There are plenty more out there, you know." The TV producer winked at Rachel and Rachel winked back.

Lucia shook her head. "I think you're dating all the eligible ones."

Rachel glanced at her watch. "Anyway, can't stop and talk men. I have to go and do what Dallas has asked me to do."

"Show wealthy women how to create complicated desserts which they'll never make?"

"Yeah, ironic really. These women hire companies like mine to cater their dinner parties."

"I guess it doesn't matter. The money they've paid to come here tonight will go to one of Dallas's charities." She sighed again at the thought of Dallas's good heart, of which few people were aware.

"Move on, girl!" Rachel took a deep breath and turned on a smile. "Okay, I'm ready. Show time! Catch you later, Lu."

Lucia watched Rachel move toward the stage prepared with the tools of Rachel's trade—mixers, chopping board, bowls, small oven—all beautifully co-ordinated with Rachel's trademark duck-egg blue range of kitchen equipment and accessories. The cameras flashed, and Rachel assumed her role of sexy celebrity chef with apparent ease.

The crowds moved in front of Lucia, and she could only hear Rachel now—the sexy voice, the banter. She was a real entertainer. But Lucia wasn't in the mood for entertainment. She glanced toward the doors which led out onto a deck which overlooked the harbor. No, she was in the mood for escape.

It was the perfect early spring evening in Wellington, Lucia thought as she walked onto the terrace that perched above the harbor. The city was still bathed in warm sunshine. The eastern hills, which lay across the water were now tinged with the warmer orange glow that showed night wasn't far away. She'd been in New Zealand for a full year now, and she still couldn't get over the difference between this friendly, compact city—where everybody seemed to know everyone else—and Shanghai, where she'd lived since she was seventeen. And she relished every detail of that difference.

Relished everything except one. She glanced inside. The sight of Dallas talking to a beautiful brunette underscored her sense of loneliness, despite all her new friends. And to top it all, he wanted to introduce her to someone. She refused to be palmed off onto some friend of her ex and had avoided him all evening. No, she was better off out here, alone.

Alone. It wasn't what Lucia wanted, and she hoped it wasn't her destiny. But after a couple of relationships in Shanghai which had gone nowhere, she was beginning to wonder. She shivered at the thought and crossed her arms.

"It's not *that* cold, is it?"

She turned to see the owner of the voice leaning against the far end of the wall, half-hidden by a pillar: his tux slung over the balustrade, the dark silk dangling carelessly over the blue water. He was tall, but not overly so, with his white shirt fitting snugly over the strong, broad build of a rugby player. Not her type, of course, but still, a girl couldn't help noticing.

She shook her head. "No, not really. Just a stray thought."

"Well, if you're going to have stray thoughts, this is the place to have them. The breeze will blow them away."

She smiled at the notion and looked at him with renewed interest. "Is that why you're here?"

"No. I'm here because I have no interest in cooking. Or parties come to that. Guess you don't either?"

"No, I like cooking, and I like parties. Usually. It's just..." She sighed, trying to figure out the source of her disengagement. "Just that I'm tired, I guess."

"And that stray thought didn't help."

Her gaze lingered on him a little longer, as she suddenly wondered if he knew about her and Dallas. But he didn't look familiar. "No, it didn't."

He pushed himself off the wall and walked toward her. He slipped his hands into the pockets of his trousers, narrowed his eyes and cocked his head to one side, as if trying to gain her measure. She looked out to the water. She didn't want him to gain her measure. Because, contrary to Rachel's suggestion, she had no interest in finding a man. She was feeling battle-weary and right at this moment reckoned "lonely" might be preferable to being hurt. Again.

"So," he said gently, as if somehow understanding her fears, "did it drift off on the breeze? That stray thought?"

She shook her head. "No, the wind's not strong enough."

"You should come in the winter then. The Wellington winds are enough to drive anything away."

"I *have* come here in winter."

"You have?"

"Yes, I work in the city art gallery as an art restorer. I'm usually stuck inside, staring at tiny flakes of paint, so I like to walk across to Te Papa and come out here after I've gone through the museum."

He turned to look across the harbor, toward the hills, echoing her stance. "I can't imagine doing something like that all day. Concentrating on one small thing for hours on end."

"When it's going well I get lost in it and forget where I am. And then I surface and find I've hardly moved all day. So I come here."

"Perfect antidote."

"Especially in winter. The southerly winds just miss this balcony. It's wonderful. Like being on the prow of a boat on a stormy sea."

He leaned against the balcony next to her. "A woman after my own heart. Nothing better than being on a boat. Do you fish?"

She grimaced. "No. I only like the thought of sailing. The closest I've come is friends' motor boats, watching fireworks in the harbor."

"Oh."

She noted the disappointed tone. "You?"

"Yeah," he said with renewed enthusiasm. "When I'm in New Zealand, I'm out on my boat every chance I get. And then, when I'm not fishing, I'm in the hills, hunting. You see the range of hills over here? On the other side of Tara Harbor? That's where I go." He pointed to the other side of the harbor where lights were beginning to brighten as the day faded.

She frowned. "Tara Harbor? You mean Wellington Harbor?"

He grinned. "It's Maori name is *Te Whanganui a Tara*, or The Great Harbor of Tara. My Maori ancestors were of the Ngai Tara tribe and my grandmother used to insist we call it that." He shrugged. "When I fly into the airport, as soon as I see the lights of Tara Harbor I know I'm home."

Home. The word struck a painful chord. It was what she'd come here to find but which remained elusive. She cleared her throat and forced a smile. "So... what is it you hunt?"

"Wild pig or deer."

"Oh, right." She wished she hadn't asked. The sense of distaste at the thought of killing something was arrested by the sight of his lightly clasped hands on the balustrade. She suddenly imagined those thick long fingers touching her, brushing her skin, discovering her... She swallowed and looked away, lifting her face to the breeze, willing it to cool the heat that had instantly ignited at the thought of his skin against hers.

"Don't suppose you hunt?" he asked.

"*Do* women hunt?"

"Now *that's* a sexist remark, which surprises me," he said in a teasing tone. "I know a lot of women who hunt."

"Well, not me. I'm a vegetarian. And, well, I don't often leave the city. Apart from my early years in Italy, I was raised in cities and feel at home in them."

He sighed and looked at the view. "Right." A small grin played on his lips as he inclined his head to hers. "Do you think we have anything in common?"

She laughed and shook her head. "Doesn't look like it."

He stepped away with a sigh. "It's not going to stop me from asking you out. Maybe we can use it as an opportunity to see if there are any interests—anything—we share."

Just in that direct approach she sincerely doubted it. The majority of men she knew were sophisticated men who rarely said anything with this man's degree of directness. He wasn't anything like the men she usually dated which, she reflected, was probably a good reason to agree.

"I don't know your name."

"Guy." He stuck out his large, capable hand. "Guy Martin."

She lifted her hand, and it was engulfed in his. His hand was warm, the pads on his palm slightly calloused—its abrasion against her sensitive hands, more used to the fine control of brushes, scrapers and cotton balls, sent shivers of electricity running through her arm. His eyes narrowed at the same time she felt the attraction zap through her, before it came to rest low in her stomach, where it remained.

"Lucia," she whispered, struggling to find her voice. "Lucia Rossi."

"Lucia," he repeated. "Beautiful. Your name sounds like the whisper of the wind in the trees."

"It's... it's the way I say it. The Italian way. My father was Italian," she added unnecessarily. What was this man about? A rugby-playing hunter with the soul of a poet? She must have looked startled because he smiled and the tension was broken.

"So, can I take you out and we can discover what else we don't have in common?"

She really shouldn't. But then, she *would* be safe. There wouldn't be any future in it, no risk to her emotions. He appeared to be the total opposite to her in every way.

"Sure. That would be nice. When and where?"

"How about now? Let's escape, get a drink and something to eat?"

Lucia felt a rush of excitement. She felt like a kid, enticed to play truant. She glanced inside. Dallas was still there, surrounded by a group of beautiful people, his usual distant self, but apparently enjoying the attention of one woman in particular.

"Sure. Why not? I'll fetch my jacket."

"I'll meet you by the exit."

She re-entered the reception feeling a different person. As she walked past Dallas, she no longer felt the sting of rejection. She ignored him and the simpering woman who was desperately trying to entertain him with some anecdote. Good luck with that, she thought, smiling to herself as she caught Dallas sighing with boredom. The man still made her laugh. His impatience and short temper were legendary, but he had a really good heart. Shame it wasn't meant for her.

He didn't notice her pass by and Rachel was still the center of attention and wouldn't be concerned by her absence. Besides, they were neighbors and would catch up for breakfast before work the following morning. She slipped into the cloakroom and retrieved her jacket. From there, she made her way toward the exit, where Guy was waiting for her.

He grinned as she approached and opened the door wide. "You came."

She stepped through the door. "I said I would."

"Yes, but I thought you might have had a change of heart after considering how little we had in common."

She raised an eyebrow. "Maybe it's exactly that which makes this so appealing right now."

They stepped out onto the broad concourse that linked

the museum and the sea to the city. "You mean, it's not my good looks or charm?"

"No. Nor your modesty either."

He laughed. "In which case, I'm pleased to be very unlike you, at this moment, if that's all I have going for me."

Despite the lack of common ground, they talked easily as they walked away from the waterfront and into the city. Lucia wondered where they were going as they passed the smart bars and restaurants she usually frequented. But, she reminded herself, it was different she'd wanted. And it looked like different was what she was going to get.

She began to have second thoughts as they walked past the busy downtown district and proceeded to a seedier part of Wellington she rarely visited. Where on earth was he taking her?

"It's here," he said, stopping beside an open door either side of which were graffitied walls and layers of bill posters. A discreet sign proclaimed it to be *Kostas*, whatever that was, and a red light glowed invitingly from within the red-tiled Victorian porch, revealing a flight of stairs leading downwards.

She smiled unsurely. "Are you sure? This looks like a strip joint."

"That's probably because it used to be."

"But it's not now?" she asked doubtfully, looking around at the peeling paint and scuffed skirting boards. "Are you sure you're not taking me to someplace where I'll be drugged and shipped off to a slave trade?"

"No, but if that's the kind of nightlife you're used to," he said, stepping away, "I'm sure I can find something along those lines."

She laughed. "I wouldn't want to put you to all that bother. This looks fine."

"Seriously, Lucia, it's more than fine; it's the best Greek restaurant I know. Friends of mine run it."

"Really? It just doesn't look..." How could she tell him that his friends ran the seediest dive she'd ever seen?

"Don't be put off by looks. There's always more to something than meets the eye."

She looked at him sharply. Wasn't that what her work was about—revealing the treasure which lay beneath the grime? "You got me there. Okay, I'm game," she said, as she took tentative steps down the wooden stairs which were worn in the center.

He pushed open another door at the bottom of the stairs, and Lucia was immediately assailed by the wonderful aroma of spices and herbs. Inside, the restaurant glowed with the rich colors of kilim rugs, strewn over the floor and seats. Above low tables, ornate copper and glass chandeliers hung, casting intimate pools of soft amber light. The whole impression was slightly chaotic, warm and inviting.

"Guy!" The owner came into the room, wiping his hands on a towel, before giving Guy a big hug. The two men laughed and exchanged insults before they were shown to a corner table. Then he looked appreciatively at Lucia.

"And what is Guy doing with such a classy lady as yourself?"

"The wind blew her to me," said Guy, before she could reply. Apparently satisfied, Kostas laughed, thumped Guy on the back, and left.

Startled, she looked into his warm eyes. There it was again, that romanticism, so at odds with everything else about him. She looked away, equally abruptly, as she tried to marry these two images in her head.

She still hadn't managed it when the first dishes were set before her.

"But we haven't ordered."

Guy laughed. "You don't order here. You get what's been made, and is the freshest."

"Is there meat?" she asked tentatively, exploring the dish with her fork.

"Not for you. I told him you were a vegetarian, he grumbled a bit, but said he'd put something together for you." He leaned forward. "See, there's no trace of meat in that dish." He helped her to some. "Try some."

She did and she immediately closed her eyes with pleasure as the flavors blended and dissolved on her tongue. She picked up her fork with renewed interest. "That was wonderful!"

"See! What did I tell you?"

Dish after dish of equally delicious food emerged from the kitchen and were quickly devoured by them both. Lucia hadn't realized how hungry she was. They were joined by other late diners, many of whom Guy knew, and the wine and conversation flowed.

As the restaurant was closing, Kostas and his chef came by with bottles of liquor. As Lucia nursed her cup of black coffee, she watched Guy exchange anecdotes with Kostas. The mischief they'd got into as university students had formed a bond between the two which obviously ran deep. There was something reassuring about seeing the affection and high esteem Guy's old friends held him in.

She wasn't sure whether it was the wine, her strong physical attraction to him, or the lure of original artwork, but, by the end of the evening, she'd agreed to visit Guy in his country home the following weekend to check out his family's collection of paintings by New Zealand artists.

She was still wondering if she hadn't been a bit rash when they emerged from the café into the Wellington streets where a light rain was falling. But any lingering doubts vanished when Guy put his jacket around her and somehow left his arm around her, too. It felt good, she thought as she drew closer. And he smelled good. Pure man with an edge of sandalwood. It made her mouth water just as much, if not more than, at dinner.

"Care for a nightcap? I know a good bar around the corner."

"Absolutely. If your taste in restaurants is anything to go by, I want to check it out."

"It's not so off the grid as the restaurant. In fact, it's here." He held open a door.

She was vaguely disappointed. She'd been here before, many times, some of them with Dallas. "Oh, sure."

"We can go somewhere else, if you prefer? Another 'seedy' backstreet, I think you called it?"

"Here's fine." She laughed as she stepped inside the bar. It was packed as usual, and they had to squeeze in.

Guy grabbed a stool. "Here, you take that, and I'll go and get us a couple of drinks. Brandy?"

She nodded. "Small one, please."

She watched him walk away, his shirt plastered wetly against his body, revealing his muscled arms and broad shoulders. She had a sudden vision of him without a shirt, his skin slick with sweat from the heat of a day's hunt. The image refused to leave.

She watched as he leaned in to shout his order to the barman, barely heard above the laughter and talk in the room, which was without the sound-absorbing furnishings that made conversation so easy in the Greek restaurant. His hair was cropped short, in a no-nonsense style, that showed his lack of interest in his appearance, but suited him. It revealed the strong shape of his head, and, as he turned to one side, the overhead bar light caught the side of his face. Her stomach did a flip of desire. His jaw formed a clear, strong line which revealed more to her than anything he could have said. It showed a stubbornness of purpose and strength which was infinitely appealing to her. She'd been drifting emotionally for so long that the thought of reaching out and clinging to something—someone—so strong and safe was very seductive. They might not share the same interests but she'd always been drawn to strong characters. A small warning bell rang.

She looked away, through the rain-streaked window out to Courtenay Place, still busy with theatergoers emerging from the theater opposite. *She* was strong and stubborn, too. Strong plus strong didn't go smoothly, she reminded herself.

"Lucia!"

She turned abruptly at the sound of her name. She knew that voice. And she was right. Walking up to her was Dallas Mackenzie, the man she'd been avoiding all night.

"Dallas." She rose in greeting, and he kissed her cheek.

"You left early, Lucia," he said reproachfully. "Why's that?"

"You *know* why, Dallas."

He sighed. "I'm sorry, Lucia, but it's for the best. I don't *do* love, and you *need* it. But not with me."

She bit her lip and half-nodded. She'd held such high hopes for Dallas Mackenzie—handsome, charismatic, with high morals and a strong connection to both the sophistication of the city and his family—but it had come to nothing. He was a serial dater, and had made it crystal clear that he wouldn't settle with one woman, ever. "Sure. It's just"—she shrugged—"it was fun."

"And we'll still see each other. Often. Just not in the

same way as we have been." He lifted her chin so she was forced to look up to him. "Okay?"

"Of course." She smiled.

"You deserve the best in life. The *best* kind of future. And I can't give you any of that."

"But—"

"No buts. I'm right, and deep down you know it."

He *was* right. And she *did* know it, particularly after spending the evening with Guy. "Okay, you've got me there. You *are* right. I know you're right. So... did you stay long?"

"Only long enough to make sure everyone had a good time."

"Yourself included," she said, unable to stop herself from having a dig at the way women flocked around him.

"What?" He looked genuinely puzzled.

She sighed. "Never mind." He was hopeless. He had the ability to ignore anything or anyone who didn't interest him. And obviously, the woman who'd been talking to him, who'd thought she'd got his attention, had been discarded with total ease.

"Hey, look, there's Guy!" Dallas turned to greet Guy and then faced Lucia. "I wanted to introduce you, but you disappeared, and then I couldn't find Guy."

Lucia frowned. Guy grinned at Lucia but didn't say anything.

"Lucia, this is Guy Martin. Just returned from overseas, and he's single."

Lucia's heart fell.

"Guy, this is Lucia Rossi. A very special lady who also happens to be single."

Guy laughed. "Still haven't figured out how to hide your intentions, have you, Dallas?"

"What's the point?"

Guy shrugged. "Maybe in case it has the opposite effect. Lucia doesn't look too happy about the 'you're both single' line."

Dallas glanced sharply at Lucia. "Why not? It's a fact. You *are* both single. And I reckon you'd get along."

Lucia was incensed. No sooner had Dallas broken up with her then he was pushing her toward the first single man who came to mind. It showed how little he thought of her. "I don't *need* setting up, Dallas!"

"It's not a setup! Think of it as an introduction. That's all it is."

"I don't *need* introductions." She glanced at Guy and felt the anger disappear. He was grinning at her and she suddenly saw the funny side. "I don't need introductions," she repeated, more quietly, "because I can tell what people are like from one glance."

"Yeah, right." Dallas took a sip of his drink. "So tell me about Guy."

Lucia narrowed her gaze, pretending to inspect Guy and nodded slowly. "He's a man of the outdoors—loves nothing more than to hunt or fish. And... I think... yes, it's a contrast to his world of business which I sense is something in the legal field. Something which takes him all around the world. I think he returns quite often to New Zealand, but not for very long at a time. And, yes, I do believe he's taken a break from his legal work to attend to his family's business."

Dallas frowned and looked from one to the other.

"And," continued Lucia, "his passion is rugby." She looked at Dallas. "How did I do?"

"You've met him already." He glanced at the two drinks which Guy held, one of which he now passed to Lucia. "So what do you think of my best buddy?"

It was Lucia's turn to frown. "Best buddy?"

"Yeah, you didn't think I was going to introduce you to anyone I didn't know well, did you? He's been my best mate since university, and he's the person I'd trust with my life." He turned to Guy. "And I have more than once, eh Guy?"

"Yeah, and if you don't do it again, that would be good."

"No worries on that score. I keep well away from trouble these days. And you always have, eh Guy?" Dallas turned to Lucia. "Guy's not like me, he's always wanted a family." He turned to Guy. "Was it ten kids you used to say you wanted?"

Guy's smile had unaccountably vanished. "That was then, not now, not anymore, Dallas. That family thing isn't for me."

Dallas looked vaguely uncomfortable, which must have been a first for him, Lucia thought, before he changed the subject.

Lucia tuned out as Dallas and Guy reminisced about the last time Guy had apparently stepped in and rescued Dallas from a mess of his own making. All she could think of was that she'd thought Guy was different. But he wasn't. For all the outward differences between him and Dallas, it seemed they both wanted the same thing—to remain single.

If she'd known that Guy was in any way connected to Dallas, she'd have run a mile. Because she didn't want another Dallas. She couldn't risk her heart with another Dallas. But she'd committed herself to visiting Guy's home to look at his paintings and there was no way she could get out of it without appearing rude.

Dallas and Guy burst out laughing as they continued to reminisce. But Lucia wasn't laughing. She'd ended up intrigued by a man just like Dallas. And that meant their relationship was doomed even before it had begun.

CHAPTER TWO

It was late morning by the time Lucia arrived at Onihau Estate, an hour north of Wellington.

She'd spent the whole week arguing with herself about whether she should go. On the one hand, she didn't want to get herself involved with someone exactly like Dallas. Then, on the other hand, she remembered the sweetness of some of Guy's words. Surely those words of poetry didn't come from a cold heart? But, whichever type of man Guy Martin was, the bottom line was that she'd promised to come and look over his art collection. And she always kept her promises.

But as she turned up the drive and stopped in front of the pillared portico and peered at the Mediterranean-style house, the truth hit her. The real bottom line was that she couldn't deny her intense attraction to him, and she was only here because she hadn't been able to think of anything else all week.

She stepped out onto the paved drive, pushed the door closed and looked around. Cicadas chirruped in the olive trees, basking in the sunshine. There was no other sound except the clatter of palm leaves shifting in the breeze and the far-off drone of a mower. It wasn't what she'd expected.

To the west lay the range of hills she'd had to cross to get here from Wellington and, to the east, she could see the distant blue of the sea. All around the house were grapevines and olive groves, as far as the eye could see. She could have been in Italy. And, for all her love of cities, she was filled with vivid memories of her early years growing up in Italy with her father and his family, before he'd died and her world had changed.

"Lucia!"

She spun round to see Guy descending the steps. He was dressed casually in shirt and jeans and she couldn't help checking him out from head to toe. She suddenly realized what she was doing and looked into his eyes, hoping like hell he hadn't noticed. "Guy!"

"How was the traffic? You really should have let me bring you over in the helicopter."

"The drive was fine, and I had work to finish last night." It was also a lie. She wanted to arrive under her own steam so she had control. If she wanted to leave, she could. Any time.

She walked to him and felt suddenly awkward. During their one evening together she'd felt incredibly close to him, but now she didn't know how to act. Luckily, he took the initiative and gave her a warm embrace and kissed both cheeks. "Welcome to Onihau. I'm glad you could make it." He opened the door wide. "Come in and have a coffee. My parents are out, but they'll be home soon, and you can meet them then."

She'd hoped Guy's parents would be around. She knew they lived there and, somehow, it made her feel safer.

"What an amazing place. It's so peaceful."

"Should be. The nearest neighbors are a half mile away."

She laughed. "I can't imagine having no one around me."

"When we're harvesting the olives and grapes, the place is full of people. Otherwise it's usually only my parents."

"You don't live here permanently?"

"No. Used to, but not anymore."

"Really? Why not?"

He shrugged. "Busy. I haven't been in New Zealand much over the past few years. And now I'm in Wellington I prefer to manage the family's property business from there. My father looks after the estate and winery here. He's had a health scare and wanted me to take some of the pressure off him. But I don't want to be out here full time." He looked around with a brief frown. "Anyway, come in, and I'll show you around."

They walked up the steps to the double doors made of oak.

"Have you had the property long?"

"My great-great-grandfather bought the land in the nineteenth century. So I guess you could say we've had it a while. He's also responsible for most of our collection of paintings. We even have a Goldie."

Lucia stopped walking. "A Goldie?"

Guy grinned. "A fake Goldie. We used to own the original but that's another story."

"Sounds intriguing."

"Ask my mother to tell you about it." He walked across the open-plan kitchen/living room to a coffee machine. "Espresso?"

"Sure. That would be great." She walked over to the French windows and looked out. "This is beautiful."

"Go outside and explore if you like. I'll bring the coffees out."

She stepped outside and once more was overcome with memories of Italy. From the terra-cotta pavers to the faded blue paint of the wooden furniture set under a shady arbor of grape vines, to the parched pale gold of the hills and the hot sun and olive trees, it was as if she'd stepped into an old life—a life where anything had been possible. She walked out from under the sheltered veranda, toward a bright blue pool. Beyond the formal gardens designed in the Italianate style, the grape vines raked across the land, trimmed at the edge by that fine blue line of the sea.

She breathed in the warm air, scented with gardenia and daphne and tried desperately not to let it all get to her. She couldn't be seduced by this dream of what she'd come to New Zealand to find. Because it was a mirage. It wasn't real. Guy didn't want a family. Guy didn't even want to live here. None of this could be hers.

"Here's your coffee."

She turned around quickly to find he'd placed the coffee and biscuits on a table under the arbor and forced herself to smile.

"You've a beautiful place here. It's a wonder you prefer Wellington."

"I used to live here, a few years ago." His expression became pensive. "But circumstances changed, and I left. It's not my home anymore."

Home. She tried not to let the word resonate in her mind. It was like a siren call to her, but one she had to ignore if she wasn't to be hurt again. She sat and took a sip of her coffee. Just how she liked it, strong and black. "So Wellington's your home now?"

"I have a place there. I guess you could call it home.

Nearest thing to it. Over the past few years, I've lived in hotels—Sydney, LA, wherever work took me."

"And that suited you?"

"Yes. Or rather it did. But I need to be in New Zealand now. Can't say I'm entirely used to the idea yet. I hate the thought of being tied down."

It wasn't news, but still, it killed any remaining dreams stone dead. Lucia was saved from answering by the sound of a car approaching.

"That'll be Mum and Dad. Come on, I'll introduce you."

Guy's father, Don, was the image of Guy and his mother, Barbara, was a sweet woman of around sixty whom Lucia took an instant liking to. As they sat and talked, Lucia soon realized that behind Barbara's quiet charm was a steeliness not unlike her own mother's. Despite Don's booming voice and liking for long, humorous anecdotes which had them all laughing, it was clear by how they acted that it was Barbara who was the force behind the marriage. And it was also Barbara who was most interested in the painting collection they'd inherited

"Don's great-grandfather began the collection," Barbara said. "He specialized in New Zealand artists—especially the ones he knew personally."

"So what's the story behind the Goldie?" asked Lucia.

Barbara glanced at Don and leaned forward to Lucia so they wouldn't be overheard. "Don has no interest in art and was worried about having such a valuable painting in the house—even though the subject is his great-grandmother. It was before we were married, and when I found out he intended to sell the Goldie to the Museum of New Zealand at a rock-bottom price, I can assure you, I hot-footed it over here. But it was too late, there was nothing I could do. At least Don had managed to include an excellent forgery in the deal." She sighed. "Of course it turns out that the dealer wasn't working for the museum after all, and when Don discovered the museum knew nothing about the sale, he tried to track down the dealer and the painting but neither were anywhere to be found."

"That's terrible!" said Lucia. "But not unheard of in the art world. People go to great lengths to own an original, especially something as precious as a Goldie."

Barbara smiled. "Yes, they do. Anyway, my dear, Guy should show you the paintings." Barbara paused, her eyes narrowing a little as she surveyed Lucia. Lucia began to feel a little unnerved. "I think you'll find them interesting. Particularly the Goldie." Barbara rose. "Guy, why don't you show Lucia the paintings while I prepare us some lunch?"

"Sure thing." Guy grinned that incredibly seductive grin that had Lucia weak at the knees, which didn't seem remotely appropriate given his parents' presence. "Would you like to see our fake Goldie, Lucia?"

"Absolutely!"

Guy led the way through the house, showing her around as they went. The new house had been built on the site of the old homestead and incorporated some of the old wood in the staircase, above the open fires and beams, giving the new house character and a connection with the land.

They walked through to the more formal areas of the house. Along the wide hallway, sheltered from the direct blast of the harsh New Zealand sun, was the gallery whose walls were lined with original paintings. Lucia stopped at each one in turn. They were all fine paintings, and, to her mind, seriously undervalued by the market. And then she turned and saw the painting at the end of the hallway and stopped in her tracks. The portrait of a beautiful Maori woman, her gaze averted, the intricacies of her feathered cloak so realistically painted, was instantly recognizable as a Goldie.

"If we'd kept the original it would have had to have been placed in the bank vault." Guy walked over to it, in pride of place, lit by one small overhead light. "But now we're the proud owners of a fake, we can keep it here." He turned to look at her. "You know? I think I enjoy it better for not being original."

Lucia walked up to it slowly. She'd seen genuine Goldies on display and had had the good fortune to work on one, so she knew them well. She'd seen this one in catalogs where it was referred to as being held in a private overseas collection.

She examined it from a distance at first before coming closer. "It's beautiful. The way he's painted her hair and hands. So detailed"—she stood back for a different perspective—"and yet so balanced." She peered more closely at the painting, scrutinizing the actual brushstrokes. She glanced at Guy who was watching her, rather than the painting. "May I touch it?"

"Be my guest."

She gently traced a brush stroke with her index finger. Then she drew closer and smelled it, her heart racing with every second that she examined the painting. And it had nothing to do with the man whose eyes she could feel on her back.

She stepped away again and turned to Guy, who was leaning against the opposite wall, his arms folded, openly watching her.

"Who declared it to be a forgery?" she asked.

Guy opened his eyes wide as if re-focusing himself. "It was a couple of men who tricked dad. I can't remember their names. They probably didn't give him the right ones anyway. They made the whole thing sound genuine—even setting up fake offices."

"Well," she said, taking one last look at the painting. "They were wrong. This is the original."

He walked over to her, his stance no longer relaxed. He looked at the painting and then to her. "It can't be."

"I think it is."

He frowned. "You think?"

"I can't be one hundred percent sure until I get it into my studio and test the paint. But I'm happy to do that, if you like."

It was shadowy in the hallway, but the light caught his bright blue eyes, in which she could read surprise, interest and doubt—all at once. He was an open book.

"Thank you. I'll check with Mum and Dad, but I'm sure they'll want to know the truth. Although..."

"Although what?"

"Although, if it is the original, then someone, some-where who believes they have the original, won't be very pleased." He grunted. "Serves them right for tricking Dad in the first place."

She shrugged. "I guess they won't be pleased. But that's immaterial. It's important to know what is, and what isn't, the real thing."

"Why?" He smiled at her. "Does it matter? We've been enjoying the painting either way."

"Of course it matters." She knew it did but, for the life of her, she couldn't express why. You knew where you were with the genuine article; it was that simple. "I'll check into it when I get back."

"Well, original or not, I can't part with it. I've got used to it being there. I say 'hi' to her as I go past. She's my great-

great grandmother; the house wouldn't be the same without her."

"There are some well-known forgeries out there. You could always replace it with one of them. Worth a fraction, but impossible to tell with an untrained eye."

"So I wouldn't know the difference?"

"I doubt it."

"Would you?" he asked softly.

"Always." She went closer and straightened the frame on the wall and stood back to admire it. "I can't bear to see an original painting sitting awkwardly on the wall. It deserves the best."

"So you don't straighten fakes, then," he said with a smile.

"Never." She grinned.

"Come on, I'll show you the others."

As Guy showed her around the paintings, Lucia became lost in a world she knew well—art. Her fears and disappointments were forgotten as the artwork drew her in, engaging her on every level. She'd studied art as a young girl in Italy, continued her studies when she was sent to boarding school in England and then, in Shanghai, there had been no question about her choice of degree. Art had remained the one constant throughout her life.

After a close examination of one particular painting, she turned to find Guy standing with folded arms looking at her with open curiosity.

"You changed when you were looking at the paintings."

She flushed with embarrassment as if she'd been caught out, her true self revealed. She shrugged. "Changed? Surely not."

"Yes, you did. You relaxed. For the first time since I met

you, you truly relaxed. Something about the art got to you. What?"

She looked at the painting she'd just been examining. "I guess I understand art in a way I don't understand so much else about life." She traced the line of a hillside with her fingertips. "I understand the lines, the flow, the colors. I even understand the canvases and the medium—oil, pastel, watercolor—the artist has used." It was hard trying to explain something she rarely had to explain before. It seemed this man picked up on something no one else had. "It's like..." She sighed and turned to him. It was no good. She had to reveal a little of herself in return for his interest. "It's like an escape from the chaos of life, into a world of order and completeness which I understand. I know this world. And I can control it."

He walked over to her, his eyes never leaving hers, showing an empathy which connected to her soul. He briefly ran his hand along her arm, before pushing his fingers through hers until they were entwined. "Maybe we've found something we have in common. A need to escape."

Before Lucia could reply, Guy tugged her hand. "Come on. I'll show you the rest of the place."

Lucia took one last look at the Goldie. She knew it was the original. She had that feeling, low in her gut. It was always the same. She responded viscerally when she recognized the brushstrokes of a master.

"What will you do when I prove it's the original?"

He shrugged. "We might just keep it here."

"It's too valuable."

"Only to us. No one will know. But, if word does get out to the person who believes they own the original, then we'll have to look into our legal position. Maybe contest the original sale."

"Hopefully, the person will be reasonable. Although the way in which they purchased it doesn't suggest they will be."

"No. But, if the worst happens and we have to return it, I'll be happy with a good reproduction."

"But it wouldn't be right!"

He shrugged. "Maybe not. But it's just a picture, isn't it?"

Lucia nearly choked. "Just a..."

"I'm not like you, Lucia. I'm not passionate about original paintings as you are. Fancy a ride out to see what I am passionate about?"

She frowned, as her mind went haywire imagining what he was passionate about, and wondering what he was about to show her.

He grinned and stepped away from her. "No need for concern. It's just a small corner of my land which has a very special place in my heart. Something of more value to me than a painting. We'll go out there and then come back and break the news to Mum and Dad about the Goldie."

She shook her head. Art was her life. But, for Guy, it was simply something pretty. He no more needed it than she needed to climb a mountain. Mountains were beautiful but alien worlds to her. He might be right, she thought—they both needed to escape into their worlds, but how different those worlds were.

They had no future, that much was clear. They both wanted completely different things. She'd enjoy today, check out his painting and then that would be that. She glanced at him and felt a sharp reaction, deep inside. So long as she remembered that.

Guy hadn't exaggerated about Onihau's remoteness. It was five minutes before they arrived at a small town where, apparently, he knew everyone. He slowed, lowered his window and waved at a mother pushing a stroller who grinned and waved back. Lucia pretended not to notice the warmth of the woman's smile. But he hadn't gone a hundred yards before he slowed his car and called out the window to an elderly couple. They exchanged pleasantries before continuing along the road. Lucia wondered if they'd get through the town without another stop. They didn't. On the edge of town, Guy pulled up again and lowered the window. He high-fived a tall Maori, dressed sharply in a business suit.

"Where've you been, Guy? Haven't you had enough of the big city yet?"

"No, not yet. Too busy."

His friend nodded, obviously understanding the situation. "And are you playing rugby again?"

"No."

"Mate! We need you. You were the best we had."

"No, can't do it. Catch up with you in the pub, eh?"

Lucia let the silence continue for some time after they drove off. But curiosity got the better of her.

"So... you said you loved rugby."

"I do. I loved to play it, and I love to watch it."

"Then... why don't you play? I don't understand. And you seem to love this place but don't come here very often."

Did she imagine it, or did Guy's hands tighten around the wheel? "I was married, Lucia."

Lucia looked sharply out the side window. As an answer to her question, it wasn't the most expected. "Was?"

"Yes. My wife died. Car accident three years back."

Ah, that would explain Dallas's gaffe the previous weekend. Typical Dallas. "I'm sorry."

"Yes. Me too. Anyway... being here... at Onihau, with the guys, it brings back too many painful memories."

She looked slowly away, suddenly understanding him. Everything fell into place. He didn't want love, he didn't want marriage and a family, he didn't want a home, because he'd had them all and, although he'd lost them, he still held them close to his heart.

There was no room for her in his world, other than as a distraction. That much was crystal clear. She'd do what she could for him with regards to the paintings, and leave it at that. They'd be friends. Nothing more.

They parked by the craggy hillside and looked up at the dark smudge six feet above the ground. "We're here."

Lucia looked at the barren-looking hillside and frowned. What was she meant to see?

"This is it?"

"You sound disappointed."

"Well no, I just imagined... something... well, a bit different."

"You *will* see something a bit different." He glanced at her feet, her perfectly painted toenails peeping from high-heeled sandals. "Don't you own any sensible footwear?"

"I don't think I've ever bought anything marketed as 'footwear' before."

He laughed. "Then you'd better tread carefully and hold on to me."

There was a part of Lucia—certainly not the sensible

part—that was glad she was wearing impractical shoes, as they walked up the path toward the smudge that she soon saw was a cave. The stone on the floor of the cave was smooth to begin with, but she still hung on to his arm, rationalizing to herself that you never knew when the path would become uneven.

"Careful around this corner. And mind your head." Away from the light at the cave's entrance, it was pitch black. He switched on a torch. "It's okay, the going's pretty smooth most of the way. It's not far now."

A wave of fear turned her forehead clammy and quickened her heartbeat. What the hell was she doing—disappearing into the black depth of a hillside with a virtual stranger? She had a sudden vision of newspaper headlines advertising her disappearance. But then he paused as if sensing her discomfort.

"We can turn back if you like?"

What man intent on murder would give her the opportunity to turn back? She looked at him in the shadows created by the torch and her nerves calmed. Despite everything, she felt safe with Guy and she trusted that feeling.

"No. I'd like to go on."

"Good. It's worth it." He tucked her arm more tightly into his, and they continued along the path, black all around them, except for the narrow torch beam that split the darkness. Suddenly he stopped. "Okay. I'm going to turn out the light now."

She gripped his arm. "What? It'll be pitch black! No, leave it on!"

"Hey, Lucia, don't worry. We're not moving anywhere."

"But why?"

"You'll see. Now, stay quiet, stay motionless."

. . .

Guy switched off the light and seconds turned into minutes as their eyes slowly adjusted to the dark.

He was glad he'd told Lucia about Hannah because there was something about Lucia that attracted him deeply, made him almost forget his intention to remain single. She was independent, compared to Hannah's clinginess, and easygoing, compared to Hannah's hot-headedness. She was also totally gorgeous, inheriting the best of both her Italian and Chinese ancestry—dark and sensual and yet also elegant and slightly aloof, as if wary of this alien world she'd found herself in.

All afternoon he'd taken every opportunity he could to breathe in her scent. To begin with, he'd assumed it was her perfume, but it wasn't artificial enough. Then, as they'd entered the cave and she'd bent her head to adjust her ankle strap, he'd thought it was the shampoo she used. It was only when she stumbled slightly, and he caught her in his arms, and she looked at him, long and slow, that he knew it was simply her. An exquisite mix of everything. And he also knew it was a fragrance he'd never get enough of.

"What—"

"Hush." He squeezed her hand. "Keep quite still and wait."

God help him, all he could do was inhale her. He moved his head slightly toward her and her hair lightly brushed his cheek, sending a shiver of need through his body.

And then it happened.

Slowly the faint lights flickered on. One by one to begin with, then small clusters burst into life. But Guy wasn't looking at them. He knew their ethereal beauty and was more interested in looking at another kind of beauty. His gut tightened as Lucia opened her mouth in a small gasp of wonder. Her head moved from one end of the cave to another, and up, her chin lifting, outlined by the light of the glowworms, as she looked to the roof of the cavern, dotted with pulsating lights.

Who moved first, Guy couldn't have said. But Lucia melted into his arms, and they stood, his arm around her, the side of her body tight against him. And, as one moment drifted into another, he swallowed and thought he couldn't ever remember feeling so... complete.

But the moment passed, like all other moments. Ridiculous! He was complete within himself. He didn't want another wife; he didn't *deserve* another wife.

He cleared his throat and moved away from her, and immediately the lights dimmed, as the glowworm larvae reacted to a possible threat and retreated into their nests. She looked at him, surprised.

"We should go," he said, and the lights lowered their intensity once more.

She looked at the lights which had revealed their magic for such a short time. He gripped her hand and they walked along the path, out toward the bright reality of daylight. He wouldn't deviate from the path he'd set himself the day he'd buried Hannah. He'd let her down, and she'd paid the consequences. He dared not risk a repeat.

Outside, in the bright midday sun, Lucia blinked and turned to him with an almost shy smile. "Thank you for sharing that. It was amazing."

"As good as art?"

"Definitely."

"I thought it must be. You had the same look about you that you had when you looked at the paintings."

"And I guess this is your kind of art—living, breathing art."

"You got it. And I think you just got me."

Lucia looked faintly startled, and Guy instantly regretted what he'd said.

"Ignore me. That place always gets to me." He looked at the outside of it. "Shame we won't own it much longer."

Her eyes widened. "No! Really?"

"We've gifted it to the Department of Conservation. It's been deemed a place of national importance." He shrugged. "It's not productive land. Best they have it."

She looked into the dark tunnel, and somehow he guessed what she was feeling. Because he was too. They'd connected in there. With a glimpse of the beauty that lay within but which couldn't be had. A beauty that was extinguished by movement or speech. Ephemeral. Just like love, he'd learned, it was a beauty that couldn't be captured because he was liable to destroy it. No, he had no future with anyone, least of all someone as lovely as Lucia.

"It's a shame," she said turning her back to the cave and looking out across the bright landscape.

"Yes, it is," he said, his eyes firmly on her.

CHAPTER THREE

L ucia held her breath as she looked through the magnifying lamp to the painting which lay beneath. With painstaking care, she swept a cotton bud over its corner. The difference was instantaneous. The depth of color was revealed by the light brush of neutralizer, exposing the lustrous oils in all their original splendor.

She let out her tightly held breath. She was ninety-eight percent sure it was the original. There was no way that forgers could have re-created the way Goldie prepared his canvas—from the Chinese white he used to prepare the surface, followed by the sandpapering to create a smooth surface, to the finished base of raw umber.

Still, ninety-eight percent wasn't good enough. She didn't want to get Guy's hopes up. She'd wait until she had the final results from the paint analysis to tell him. Meanwhile, the secret was safe here.

She glanced at her watch. Time she was gone. She put the painting into the safe, turned out the light and left the gallery.

She walked across the Civic Square and along the

waterfront. The harbor was dotted with white-topped waves and the Eastbourne Ferry dipped and rose in the choppy sea. She twisted her long hair into a knot to keep it out of her face as she walked the short distance past Te Papa on to her apartment.

As her mind drifted to her default dream of the past week—Guy—she found herself walking more quickly. He'd been in Sydney, Australia, all week negotiating a property deal, but had phoned and texted her a few times, and had arranged to show her around the Wairarapa region the following weekend. Just as a friend, she reminded herself. He simply wanted to take her out as a way of repaying her for the work she'd done on the painting. Simple.

Guy obviously didn't want a relationship, and therefore she didn't either. Not with him. Not with anyone who didn't want to settle down and have all the things she saw around her—a husband, children if she could, and a home. Rachel might think her unreasonably focused on kids, but she didn't see the point in being any other way. She was twenty-eight and knew what she wanted.

She took the elevator to her penthouse apartment with its 360 degree views of the harbor and, behind, to the city. She placed her bag on the kitchen bench and poured a glass of water and looked out across the harbor. She'd found her new home, that was for sure. From the moment she'd set foot on New Zealand soil, she'd felt she belonged. The feeling was only confirmed when the taxi had wound its way from the airport to Wellington, along the harbor shore. It had been a bright, clear day and she'd felt hope for the first time in a long time.

And things had fallen into place as if affirming that initial sense of hope. She'd been granted a permanent work permit as art restorer for Wellington city's art gallery and found this beautiful apartment in the same building as Rachel's. And then she'd found Dallas who'd widened her new circle of friends. And, while Dallas hadn't been the one, she knew he'd always be there for her, as a friend. And, with equal confidence, she knew that Wellington would always be her home.

She sighed and poured the rest of the water into the sink. All things considered, she was doing fine and had a lot to be thankful for. When she recalled her last few months in Shanghai, she felt the grief wash through her. She gripped the edge of the marble bench, willing its chill depth to cleanse away the memories. If it hadn't been for Rachel's friendship and suggestion to move to New Zealand, she didn't know what she'd have done. She took a deep breath as she drove down the sense of desolation.

She forced herself to think about the here and now. She was thousands of miles and a whole year from that world, that memory. She had a weekend ahead of her with a man she couldn't stop thinking about, despite her best efforts. No, she'd enjoy the weekend, she'd finalize the painting's provenance, and then she'd keep her distance from Guy.

Even as the sensible voice spoke inside her, a very un-sensible part of her felt excited at seeing him again.

She quickly changed, grabbed an overnight bag and was downstairs in the marble foyer as Guy stepped in. Her heart did a little flip.

"Lucia." He smiled and kissed her cheek, just as you would an acquaintance in Europe where he spent so much time, she said firmly to herself. "Busy week?"

"Yes. But I've found time to work on your Goldie. I'm waiting for some results, and then I should be able to give you a definite answer."

They walked outside toward his car. "So what do you think so far?"

"I haven't seen anything to change my mind. I'm sure it's the original."

He laughed. "My parents *will* be surprised, seeing as how they thought they'd sold it. I wonder what happened there? Maybe the buyers didn't know one from the other." He shrugged. "Who knows?" He looked out toward the skyline which was bright blue. "Believe it or not, there's meant to be a storm sweeping in later. Do you still want to go to the Wairarapa's south coast?" He opened the car door for her.

"Oh." She couldn't prevent the disappointment from edging into her tone. She hadn't realized that she'd been so looking forward to a day exploring somewhere she'd never been, until it looked like she might not be going. She lifted her foot to show off her new acquisition. "I've even gone and got some appropriate 'footwear'."

Guy looked at the flimsy flat shoe in designer leather— she really couldn't bring herself to get a training shoe, not when she wasn't training for anything, nor ever intended to —and laughed. "I guess as you've got your hiking boots on, we'll risk the weather."

She stepped into the car, and he closed the door behind her. She watched him walk around to the driver's seat and wondered how she could have persuaded herself she'd be safe with this man, that their relationship would be entirely platonic. He was handsome, sexy and... a total gentleman. As they drove off, the sports car roaring down the road, she couldn't help wondering if he'd be such a total gentleman in every situation.

An hour later and she'd got her wish. The beach was deserted except for a small colony of seals. Lucia even saw a couple of little blue penguins on a craggy outcrop of the cliffs that rose vertically above the sweep of sand dunes. Somehow her hand had slipped into Guy's and they'd walked for miles along the wind-swept sandy beach, barely meeting a soul.

"Is it as you imagined?" asked Guy.

"Better. I was brought up in Italy and went to boarding school in England and neither place had coastlines like this. It's so raw here. So unspoiled."

"Italy? England? I thought you lived in Shanghai."

"I lived with my father and his family until I was old enough to go to boarding school. After that, I returned to Italy only for holidays. Then, when I was seventeen, my father died. So after I left school, I went to Shanghai to be with my mother." She paused. "She left my father and me when I was six. She took my little brother with her."

He stopped walking, and she jerked to a halt, too. "Six? Your mother left you when you were only six years of age?"

"Yes."

"But you saw her regularly, right?"

"Once a year to begin with and then"—she shrugged—"after I was at school in England, less often. Mother was either busy or my father wanted me in Italy. But we used to call and then Skype regularly." She gave a small smile. "It was a shock when I moved to Shanghai at eighteen, after Father died, to see that she was a real person, moving around, not simply sitting and facing the computer screen."

Guy tightened his hold of her hand. "I can't even begin to imagine what that was like for you."

"My father barely talked about Mother and didn't like me to. So I learned not to show my feelings. After I'd finished Skyping Mother, I'd go to my room and cry. Then I'd emerge and we'd just get on with things."

Guy shook his head in disbelief. "She abandoned you both and you 'just got on with things'?"

She felt irritated at the implied rebuke. "What else do you expect a child to do?"

He shrugged. "I don't know. Maybe have a tantrum or three?"

As they walked on she wrestled with whether to tell him how she felt, how she *still* felt.

"No. No tantrums. At least not outside my bedroom. It *was* what it *was*. My mother wasn't maternal."

He snorted. "That must be the understatement of the century."

"She's told me since that she fell pregnant by accident, that she'd never wanted a child. And then, with one, she thought she might as well have a second. But it had been a mistake." She grimaced. "My brother and I were both mistakes, it seemed. But, in Italy, Mother was like a square peg in a round hole. Totally unsuited to domestic life. I only truly realized just how different her world was when I saw her in China. She is a very successful art dealer but doesn't have a maternal bone in her body."

"So how did your brother get on, and why did she take him, and not you?"

Lucia was silent, as she was deluged by the sadness and despair that his question had prompted.

"Lucia?"

She cleared her throat. "It got complicated just before she left. My father didn't take it well. Nor did I. I can hardly remember it all. But the upshot was that Roberto went with Mother, but Mother was busy and he got in with the wrong company when he hit his teens." She paused. "He died recently."

"I'm sorry."

"Yeah." She managed a brief smile. "Me too."

"You can tell me about it if you'd like?"

"No, not yet. Maybe at some point." Her brother's death was too painful for her to discuss easily. She hadn't even told Dallas everything that had happened. "Anyway, Mother and I get on pretty well now. She could relate to me as an adult. So"—she shrugged—"I'm now her beloved daughter."

"She abandoned you at six, and now you're her beloved daughter. How does that make you feel?"

"I'll never feel it's fine, but there's no point raking over the past." She shrugged.

He stopped in his tracks then, looked into the darkening sky and sucked in a harsh breath. He took both her hands in his, his eyes earnestly searching her own. "Have you listened to yourself recently? The woman abandoned you, and you insist on being reasonable."

"There's no point in being otherwise."

"Okay." He reached out and drew back the strands of hair that had escaped her band and which were blowing horizontal in the wind, and kept his hand lightly pressed to her head. With his other hand, he lifted her chin until her face was close to his. "Now tell me again... how do you *really* feel?"

Tears pricked her eyes. She tried not to think about it, to never let herself dwell on things denied her. It was history, right? What was the point?

"How do you feel?" he repeated.

She licked her lips that tasted of the salt that filled the turbulent air. "Honestly?" She closed her eyes. "Okay.

Abandoned, still. Still a little bit broken." She opened her eyes again, this time refusing to look away from his intense gaze. "A bit scared of opening up to anything, *anyone*, who might leave me again."

He shook his head slowly. "You're *so* scared. I could see it in your eyes the moment I first saw you."

She shook her head. "No. Impossible. I... I hide my feelings. No one—"

He pressed his finger lightly against her mouth. "Don't protest. I know what I saw."

She hesitated. Part of her didn't want the conversation to go down that track, but part of her was seduced by the thought of Guy seeing her for who she was, truly understanding her. "And what did you see?"

"A beautiful woman who was hurting inside... hurting so much that that hurt had become a part of her that she scarcely acknowledged anymore, probably didn't even know was there. That's what heartache is like, isn't it Lucia? It worms its way in until it becomes a part of everything you do."

Before she could answer, he kissed her, with a touch so gentle and yet so powerful that the shadows of fear and hurt that formed a hard, tight ball deep inside her, softened and dissipated for a moment.

When he pulled away, she felt herself sway toward him, not wanting the warmth and tenderness to leave her. He smiled and swept his thumb across her lips.

"I'm sorry. I'm a creature of impulse. If I see hurt, I want to kiss it better. Did I succeed?"

She swallowed, trying to shift her focus away from his lips and back to reality. His hand still lingered on her cheek, and she placed hers over it and smiled. "What hurt?"

He laughed as he put his arms around her and pulled

her to him until her cheek was pressed against his shoulder and all she could feel was the fine cotton of his shirt, all she could smell was him—a blend of fresh salty air, aftershave and something that was mouthwateringly, pure *him*. But more than that was the feeling she was in the right place. That knot inside was easier now than it had ever been. There, with the strengthening wind whipping her hair out of her ponytail, the sea spray filling the air, and the sand stinging her ankles, she felt at peace for the first time in forever.

Too soon, he pulled away. "We have to go."

"Truly?"

"Yes, look at the sky."

She turned to see a leaden sky slowly spreading from the north and the sea churning angrily.

Spots of rain began to fall. He took her hand, and they ran across the sand toward the car park, as the rain intensified. He pointed toward a low-lying hotel situated above the dunes, surrounded only by a few holiday homes.

"We'll sit this out in the hotel."

"Good idea!"

They ran up the wooden steps to the veranda, looked at each other and laughed. They were both soaked. Still smiling, they entered the warm hotel bar.

"I think we've entered another world!" exclaimed Lucia, looking around at the memorabilia that hung around the room, products of a bygone age.

"Lake Ferry Hotel used to be a popular holiday spot in Victorian times." They walked through to the bar, full of history, from its pre-loved furniture to the undulating scrim which still decorated the wall. "A ferry used to cross the lake. Now it's more of a bar for day trippers, with a few rooms for fishermen. I've stayed here a few times with my mates when the kahawai were running." He looked up as the barman approached. "Two coffees, please. And some towels." He grinned.

"Towels and coffees coming right up!"

Lucia slicked her wet hair from her face and plucked at her soaking clothes. "I can't sit around in these. I've got a change of clothes in the car. I'll just go—"

"No, you won't. I'll go."

And before she could remonstrate, he'd gone. She watched him run through the rain-lashed carpark to his car.

He returned with two bags and water dripping onto the unpolished wooden floor. His clothes clung and it was all Lucia could do to raise her eyes from his body, to which his clothes molded, revealing his impressive physique.

She passed him a towel. "I'll change in the ladies' restroom."

She changed as quickly as she could, and dried her hair with a towel. She grimaced as she looked in the mirror. There was nothing of the sleek perfectionist about her now. The clothes she'd packed for a stay at Onihau had been casual jeans and t-shirt, and her hair was a mess. She wiped away the makeup which had run and raked her hair from her face with her fingers. It was the best she could do. She'd left her bag with makeup and comb in the car. She couldn't ask Guy to make another trip.

By the time she emerged Guy was seated, looking at the menu. Somehow he managed to look even sexier with his wet, tousled hair, and his white shirt, undone at the collar and the dark business suit he'd brought with him. "Just as well I've a meeting first thing Monday morning, or I wouldn't have had any spare clothes with me. I'd have had to wait until we reached Onihau." He glanced out the window. "And that could be hours yet, judging by these clouds."

———

By late afternoon the rain was still pouring. The talk had flowed as easily as the coffee and wine which accompanied a surprisingly delicious seafood lunch.

"Come on, we'd best get to Onihau."

They went to settle the bill at the bar and got talking to the bartender.

"On the Martinborough road? You won't get through. It's closed because of a couple of mudslides."

"How long do you reckon it'll take to clear?"

He shrugged. "The digger will have to clear the Featherston slide before it gets to the one closest to us. My guess would be that it won't be opening today."

Guy and Lucia looked at each other. "Those rooms?" asked Lucia.

Guy turned to the bartender. "Don't suppose you've a couple of rooms free?"

"One left. With twin beds, I think..." The barman frowned. "Yeah, either twins or double."

"Is that okay, Lucia?" asked Guy.

She shrugged. It would have to be. "Sure. It's either that or spending the night in the car." She smiled. "I'll take a bed any day."

The manager pulled out a register and key. "It's yours."

The wine hadn't been high in alcohol, but Lucia certainly felt light-headed as she walked down old-fashioned corridors, lined with oil paintings from a different era, showing the hotel in its heyday. Light-headed and a bit giddy. She never felt giddy, she thought to herself in faint surprise. But now she did. She grinned because she simply didn't care to control her giddiness. It seemed the "sensible" Lucia had disappeared the moment Guy's lips had met hers.

And now, as Guy reached out and pushed the key into the lock, his arm brushing hers, she knew she was in big trouble. He'd totally undermined any sense of self-preservation with his charm and attention. Plus, she simply couldn't take her eyes off his body. All she wanted to do was touch it.

She tore her gaze from it now and looked up into his eyes, eyes which seemed to know exactly which way her thoughts had strayed. If the twitch of the lips hadn't given it away, the knowing look would have done. His eyes never left hers as he waited for Lucia to enter.

The room was small but clean and full of quirky character. The bed was a small double covered with a crisp white duvet and lace-trimmed pillow cases. Fluffy towels were laid on the chest that ran along the bottom of the bed. "Hey, it's nice!"

"Don't sound so surprised. We *can* do nice out here in the sticks."

He tossed the keys onto the nightstand and followed her over to the window. She leaned against the window frame through which they could see the storm-lashed sea, between the rivulets of rain that ran down the pane.

"Not exactly five-star luxury, though," he added.

She turned to face him. "It's fine." She ran her hand across the crisp linen. "It may be an old building but it's certainly cared for and well equipped. Don't worry, I'm cool with it."

"I'll sleep on the floor."

At that moment a stronger gust hit the building, causing the sash windows to rattle in their frames and a draft to blow up from between the bare boards. He frowned, and she shook her head. "You'll freeze. Besides, why would you sleep on the floor when there's a perfectly good bed ready and waiting?"

His smile was slow at first. "Because you'll be in it?"

She walked toward him, but stopped at the bed and sat on it. She bounced gently on it before turning to him. "Yep, as I thought. It's comfortable." She patted the space beside her. "Come and check it out, if you like?"

He cocked an eyebrow and walked over to her and sat beside her. He bounced once. "Um, you're right. It *is* comfortable. But perhaps we should try it out a bit more." He stood and then sat more heavily on the bed, making her bounce and fall toward him. She laughed but the laughter melted from her lips when he caught her in his arms, and she couldn't have moved away, even if she wanted to. And she definitely didn't.

It was she, this time, who kissed him. As before, her consciousness of what was around her dwindled into darkness. All her focus was on his lips moving against hers, the feel of his tongue running the length of her lips before she opened her mouth for him.

Time stood still, the rest of the world receded, and Lucia's sensible side was nowhere to be found, as the kiss deepened and swept away any last vestiges of doubt. She wanted him.

She pushed her hands under his shirt, up and around his back, her fingers smoothing over every hollow and taut muscle.

His breathing was coming hard when he pulled away suddenly. "Are you sure, Lucia?"

"Sure, I'm sure." It was all she could do to frame the words. She only had one thought, and that was seeing Guy without his clothes on. Slowly she rose and held out her hand. "Guy?" she said, unable to suppress a smile at his frown.

"But I don't have any protection."

There was no need for him to worry and she'd tell him later, but not now. Now wasn't the time for talk. Now was the time for him to give her what she wanted. She decided distraction was the best tack.

His frown proved fleeting as she moved her hands over his bare back and lifted her lips to his once more. They were soon lost in each other—lost to thought, and alive only to the sensuous thrill of exploring each other's body, of taking each other closer to finding that ultimate bliss of sensation.

It wasn't until some time later, as she lay snuggled in his arms, regaining her breath as she looked out at the stormy night, Lucia had the strange thought that she'd found something more than sensation in his arms. She frowned as she tried to analyze how she felt. Then she grunted as she realized what the strange sensation was. She felt as if she'd come home.

At the sound, Guy turned to her and kissed her, obviously mistaking her grunt for anxiety.

"Hey, I'm so sorry, Lucia. I should have had more control. We should get you an after-sex pill, to make sure you don't fall pregnant."

She kissed him and ran her finger across his lips which had given her such pleasure. "I won't fall pregnant. Not that easily anyway. I've been diagnosed as infertile, although my doctors say it's not impossible I can fall pregnant, just extremely unlikely. So... you're safe."

He frowned and gently smoothed her hair from her face. "I'm sorry. That must be hard for you."

"It's just one of those things."

"No." He shook his head. "Don't do that 'reasonable' thing with me. It's not 'just one of those things'. It's a big thing, and it hurts—I can see it in your eyes."

She closed her eyes briefly. "You see too much, Guy Martin. I'll have to wear glasses."

He smiled and passed her her sunglasses. "So long as that's all you're wearing."

She wriggled closer to him, her hands exploring all the parts of his body she'd imagined all week. He rolled on top of her and kissed her, and she grinned as she realized that once was obviously not going to be enough for either of them.

"You, Lucia, are proving to be totally irresistible."

The next morning, Lucia sighed with deep satisfaction and rolled over to face Guy who lay looking up at the ceiling, frowning.

"What's the matter?" she asked.

"I should have bought condoms with me."

"I told you, it's fine. I had a bungled operation on my abdomen in Italy. The doctors in Shanghai said the scarring is extensive and will prevent me from falling pregnant easily."

"Easily?"

"Without fertility treatment."

"Good."

She frowned. "So... children, Guy. Do you want them?"

"Me?" He shook his head and rested it on the pillow. "No. No way. Maybe..." He glanced at her, and ran his fingertips along the length of her back, making her shiver with anticipation.

"Yes?" she asked, too eagerly, wondering if perhaps he did want them eventually, just not now.

"Maybe, with you not being able to have children, and me not wanting them, we've found something we have in common." He smiled, but she didn't.

She lay on the bed, looking at the molded plaster ceiling, filled with disappointment.

"No. Not being able to have them isn't the same as not wanting them." She paused. "I *want* children. I'm looking into adoption. If I marry, I'll try fertility treatment. I'd do anything to have them."

"Oh." She heard the deflation in his voice. "I see. That is... another difference between us then."

She felt his disappointment, saw it, read it in his movements as he swung his feet out of bed and began to get dressed. And she knew by the pain she felt that she'd got in too deep already. She'd thought she could do this. Have a relationship without getting hurt, but she'd been wrong. She couldn't. What he meant was that it was one difference too many. It was a deal breaker.

He turned and grinned briefly, too hesitantly to be reassuring. "Would you like to carry on to Onihau as planned?"

She rose and pulled a throw around her to cover her nakedness. After a night of making love, now she wanted to hide. But she needed to know for sure how he felt. She'd give him one more chance to let her know whether he was still interested. "You don't want to, I take it?"

She couldn't meet his gaze, but walked to the bathroom instead. She paused, waiting for his answer.

"Of course. That was what we'd arranged."

She'd have accepted any other answer but that. But there was nothing in his words, or his tone or his manner to suggest he wanted to continue the weekend.

"Um, no." She wound her hair into a knot before turning to him, focusing on making sure her face was a cool, impassive mask. "Probably not. I've got a stack of things to do in Wellington."

She didn't wait to hear his reply but entered the bathroom, closed the door and switched on the shower. She sat in a chair and put her head in her hands. How the hell had she got herself into this mess?

***

They exchanged pleasantries on the way to Wellington as if they were total strangers.

When he stopped the car in front of her apartment building, he turned to her. "Am I going to see you again, Lucia?"

"I think it's unlikely, don't you?"

"Was it that bad?"

She shook her head, not wanting to remember just how good it was. "You know it's nothing to do with the night we spent. That was... amazing. But I want an entirely different future. And it's not fair on either of us to pretend otherwise. Is it?"

For once, she couldn't read what was in his eyes. Maybe regret, maybe frustration, maybe just plain relief. Whatever, he turned away from her with lips firmly pressed together and looked straight ahead. "Sure, if that's what you want."

She swung her feet out of the car but hesitated before getting out. She reached out and rested her hand on his arm. "I think it's what we both *need*."

He didn't look at her but nodded, and she sighed and got out the car.

"Look, Guy, I'm sorry, truly sorry."

"What for?"

"That you mistook me for someone like yourself. But I want more, and you don't. And I'm done with starting relationships hoping things will change—hoping people will change—because they don't."

She closed the door before he could reply and walked away. She didn't think she could cope with prolonging the scene. She liked him. *Really* liked him, but she couldn't risk watching that "like" turn into a whole lot more, only to have him walk away, leaving her exactly where she was before —alone.

CHAPTER FOUR

"It's been over two months since I've even spoken to her," said Guy with a frustrated sigh. "I don't know why you still insist we should make it up."

Dallas finished checking over a list and handed it to the waiter with a nod of approval. He glanced at Guy who sat in one of the antique chairs, tapping the scrolled arm with irritation.

Dallas checked his phone and answered an urgent text with a one-word reply—"no". "If you weren't both so bloody stubborn you'd see I'm right."

Guy grunted. "Anyhow, I don't see why you're telling *me* all this. It's Lucia who finished it."

"Before it had even begun." Dallas sighed. "She's too scared, that woman."

Guy frowned. "Yeah, I gathered that much."

Dallas looked at him with sharp eyes. "She's scared of being hurt. And I hope you haven't done that."

Guy jumped up and walked over to the French windows which opened out onto the manicured lawns of Government House. "Of course not." He didn't like to think of Lucia hurt even though there was nothing he could do about it. Not without going against everything he'd sworn off since Hannah. "But maybe she's right. Maybe it *was* better to cut our losses early, before it got serious."

Dallas narrowed his gaze. "No, Guy, she's *wrong*. Because I *know* you both, and I *know* you'd be good together."

"Lucia and I want different things. What's the point in dating someone when there's no long-term future?"

"What's the point in living when you're going to die?" Dallas said acerbically before checking another incoming text. He dealt with it in his usual perfunctory manner and turned to Guy. "It's your damn pride that's hurting, that's all. Lucia gave you the push, and you're too proud to try to patch it up."

Dallas's phone sounded, and he grunted with irritation. "Yes?"

Guy turned to survey the lawns again, gloomily. Dallas was only half right. There was a whole lot more hurting than his pride. Lucia had got to him in a way that no one had since Hannah. But Hannah was very different to Lucia. Lucia was an independent woman, as well as a beautiful and intelligent woman—a totally mesmerizing woman. The moment she'd walked out onto that balcony he'd been shocked by the intensity of his reaction. It was as if he hadn't been alive before that moment. He hurt all right. He hurt everywhere.

"So tell me again what you fell out over."

Guy turned to see Dallas cut short his phone call and give him his full attention. And he knew then, that he didn't stand a chance. No one did, facing the full blast of Dallas's focus.

"Children. She wants them, even..." He hesitated, not knowing if Dallas was aware of Lucia's fertility issues.

"Even if she may not be able to have them. I know. It's tough on her. She'd make a brilliant mother and wife. And her urge to be both is understandable after what she's been through."

Guy frowned and turned to meet Dallas's glare. "You mean her abandonment by her mother?"

"And the rest. She had a rough time in Shanghai. Let's leave it at that. I found out about it when I was checking her out."

"You check out your girlfriends?"

Dallas looked surprised. "Of course I do. Anyway, she wouldn't elaborate, but it obviously left a mark on her."

"Tell me."

Dallas narrowed his eyes in concentration. "'Triads' bloody clash' was the sensational headline, as I remember it. But what caught my attention was the name Luli. If it hadn't been for that I wouldn't have read on."

"Luli?"

"Lucia's Chinese name. The name her mother calls her. She let it slip once."

"So what about... Luli?"

"Her brother was killed, among others, when they went to avenge some attack, or some affront or other. Lucia wouldn't tell me the details."

"But weren't the details public knowledge?"

"No. These are the Chinese Triads we're talking about. All I can assume is that her brother was involved in them in some way."

"No wonder Lucia wanted to escape Shanghai! New Zealand must feel like a walk in the park after that!"

"Precisely. She wants a peaceful life. She hates violence, understandably."

Guy suddenly remembered her flinching when he'd told her about his hunting, and nodded. "Of course."

"So she didn't mention anything about her life in Shanghai to you?"

"No."

Dallas shrugged. "Well, she didn't tell me any more than what is public knowledge. She's pretty secretive, presumably over the Triad connection. But I don't think her mother's abandonment helped her any. She's scared of being hurt, I guess. And that's why you'll be good for her. She needs someone kind and caring. She needs the kind of life you can give her."

"Are you sure about that?"

"One hundred percent. You're still hurting after Hannah, but it's time to move on. You want children, you *know* you do. Why the hell you told her you didn't is beyond me."

"Maybe, because I *don't* want children?" Guy was beginning to get irritated by Dallas now.

Dallas pressed his lips together in a firm line. "Okay, have it your way." He swept up his phone and slipped it in his pocket. "I'm not arguing over this. I've an art exhibition to host, and you have the governor-general to charm. It's why I need you on this committee. And it's why I want you to work closely with another committee member on my charitable trust."

Guy fell into step beside Dallas as they walked through the mansion house. "Can't see why you can't do both."

Dallas shot Guy a sharp glance. "Because I *have* no charm—"

"That's true enough—"

"And you've got more than your fair share." Dallas opened the door to the elegant reception room and paused. "Although it's not doing you much good at the moment. It's about time you stopped punishing yourself over Hannah's death and moved on. Maybe then you'd realize that you and Lucia want the same things out of life."

Dallas immediately took control of the room, greeting the Governor-General of New Zealand and guests to the charity exhibition of paintings he'd organized, in an attempt to loosen the pockets of the Wellington wealthy. Guy did his duty by smoothing over the troubled waters Dallas left in his wake, and charming the governor-general. Luckily, she was called away after a while and Guy moved to the open windows and looked out onto the gardens, a soft dusky purple in the deepening evening light.

He needed time to think over what Dallas had said to him. Dallas could be a complete and utter bastard but he'd always been a good friend to him, always telling him the truth, even if that truth was unpalatable.

No, he didn't want to marry on the rebound, and no, he didn't want children immediately. But long term? He couldn't imagine himself anywhere other than Onihau. And, if he was truthful, he couldn't imagine himself living alone. He couldn't imagine the gardens without a child on his old swing, without the splash and shout of kids in the swimming pool. But how could he contact Lucia again when he wasn't even sure if she was simply making excuses to end their relationship, even before it had begun?

"Lucia!"

Guy swung around to find Dallas greeting Lucia who had entered the reception room.

"I'm sorry I'm late," she said.

"No problem. In fact"—Dallas turned to look at Guy—

"I reckon you're right on time. Guy!" Guy scowled. "Come and meet the other member of the committee who you'll be working closely with."

Lucia somehow managed to keep her features in order. Unlike Guy, who could barely conceal his anger. Dallas had duped them both.

She touched Dallas's arm. "Dallas, there seems to have been some mistake. It's obvious Guy isn't thrilled to see me. I'll go. Why don't you find someone else to sit on your committee?"

She turned but Dallas reached out and grabbed her hand. "Hey, don't go, Lucia. I need you two to work together on this. There's no one else I want. And no one else better to help with this kind of thing." He gestured toward where the exhibition of New Zealand artists was still in full swing.

She narrowed her eyes.

"Just think, Lucia," Dallas continued, ignoring, or not noticing her subtle messages. "All that money that's being raised in there, and my contribution—it needs to be spent wisely, and unless I have my trusted friends at the helm, it could all go wrong. Those little people—"

"They're usually called children," interjected Lucia.

"Yes, those little people—*children*—will suffer. So, what do you say?"

He *had* to mention children, hadn't he? He was such a bastard. He knew she couldn't turn her back on something like this.

"I say," she said slowly, looking at Guy, "that if Guy is okay with this, then I am, too." She gave Guy a challenging stare.

Dallas smiled, as if he'd expected Lucia's reaction, and looked at Guy. "Well?"

Guy shot Dallas a dirty look and shrugged. "If it's okay with Lucia, then, of course, it's okay with me."

Dallas beamed. "Excellent. Out you go, then. There are people to extract money from and only you, Lucia, with your knowledge of art, and Guy—with his, whatever it is that he has—can do it."

Dallas walked away and was immediately stopped by a woman. Lucia watched, shook her head and turned to Guy.

"Dallas has pulled some low punches in his time, but this must be one of his worst," Guy said, thrusting his hands in his pockets and scowling after Dallas.

"Worst because you'll be working with me? I'm sorry that appears to be such bad news for you, but I'm not exactly thrilled, either."

"No, I guess not. After all, it was you who finished it."

"Because you'd made it crystal clear that you saw no future with me."

"I..."

Guy looked confused and uncomfortable. Lucia decided to take pity on him. "We don't have time to argue. Let's go and do what Dallas wants us to do and make this auction happen for him."

She didn't wait for Guy, but walked into the formal drawing room, which had been turned into an art gallery for the evening, and began networking.

Dallas had connections throughout Wellington—from its political elite, through to the business and artistic communities—and it seemed he'd invited them all. Normally Lucia enjoyed these events, but she was acutely aware of Guy's position in the room as she talked to potential buyers about the paintings.

Paintings she could handle—just like the art-restoring work she'd thrown herself into these past months. She knew that, understood it, and it didn't let her down. Unlike men.

She glanced across at Guy. He was standing in front of one of the most expensive paintings in the auction. And, with its abstract imagery, one of the least understood. He was talking to a man and, from what she could hear, it sounded like they were talking more about rugby than the paintings. Beside them were a very well-dressed, distin-guished-looking couple who regarded the painting with a puzzled air.

The woman asked Guy a question and Guy frowned, shrugged, and turned once more to the man to continue his conversation about rugby. The couple moved away.

She remembered what he'd said about his own artwork. He liked paintings to look like things he knew. He didn't like to guess. And one look at the painting by the artist she knew well, made her take pity on him.

"Lucia." Guy looked around as she approached as if he'd been as aware of her movements as she'd been of his. "I'd like to introduce you to Bob Whelan, he owns the Rugby Sevens and is here because..."

"Not because I'm interested in art, that's for sure," Bob said with a wide grin.

"Lucia knows all there is to know about art," said Guy, almost proudly, thought Lucia.

"I don't know that I know *all* about art. But I can help you with this particular artist. He's a highly regarded New Zealand artist, whose work is currently achieving the highest prices we've ever seen."

Bob suddenly looked interested. "What, that bird, plummeting from the sky? That's worth something?"

"Absolutely."

"I can't see it myself."

Another couple came up when she began to talk, describing what made the painting so important.

"It's similar to the style used by the Chinese artist Hua Tunan."

"You know about Chinese art, too?"

"Yes, my family in Shanghai owns some pieces which are on display in the city museum. Perhaps you'd like to see this one, over here. Here"—she gestured toward the red, stylized bird plummeting backward against a dark gray sky —"the painting references Maori myth. Transformation." She took the couple over to the next painting, leaving Guy and Bob behind, and talked them through the symbolism.

Lucia was satisfied when the couple made a mark in their program against the painting and they all moved on to the next one where she was introduced to more people.

The auction began, and people drifted toward the front of the room, leaving Lucia at the rear. As she watched the popular entertainer auction each painting, her mind wandered.

Why did all the men she was attracted to *not* want to settle down? Was it her? Or was she attracted to men who were too strong, too independent, or simply too selfish to share their future with someone?

She didn't know, but was beginning to question her own dreams. After all, if she did meet a man who wanted to marry, commit to her long term, the chances were that someone like that would want children. And that ruled her out—unless he was open to fertility treatment... or adoption... or had children of his own. Or maybe she should simply choose the adoption route. And then go with the flow—go out with the men who lived for the present, and enjoy them. All she had to do was make sure she didn't lose her heart to them. Ha! It was that simple—and that difficult.

Then the painting she'd been talking about came up. It represented transformation which was the one thing she wanted, more than anything—to leave her past behind her, and to be transformed into a different woman. But maybe life wasn't like art; maybe she was after the impossible. Maybe she should simply accept what she could get. She sighed. So many "maybes" when all she wanted was certainty.

She watched the couple she'd been talking to about the painting, but they didn't move. Instead a bid came from where Guy was standing. It was the rugby club owner with no interest in art. Lucia sighed. Seems her knowledge of art was trumped by Guy's "whatever it was" that he possessed, which Dallas couldn't put a name to. But she could. He was down-to-earth, *real*. And people understood that.

The auction wound up, and people began to drift away. Lucia turned to the paintings. She'd wait until the last of the VIPs had left and then she'd slip away.

She stepped away from one of the paintings and bumped into someone.

"Sorry!" she said spinning around to find Guy looking at her with an embarrassed smile. "Oh!" She jumped in surprise.

"Sorry to startle you."

"How long have you been standing behind me?"

"Just a few seconds."

She raised an eyebrow. "I thought you'd have gone by now. Taken the first available opportunity to leave. After all, our official duties are over."

"No, not yet. Thought I'd hang around."

"What for? I wouldn't have thought these sort of paintings interested you."

"They don't. You don't have to like them to be interested in them." He indicated the man he'd been talking to earlier who'd given the winning bid. "Take him. I told him it was the most expensive and that was all he needed to know."

She smiled and shook her head. "Of course. Well done. Mission accomplished. But you haven't answered my question—why are you still here?"

He shrugged, a small smile playing on his lips. "Maybe because I'm trying to figure out how to apologize to someone."

His smile was too rueful and engaging not to respond to. She failed to prevent a smile. "Perhaps if you tell me what happened, maybe even who the person is, I can help?" She raised a questioning eyebrow.

"Perhaps you can. You see, it's like this. After my wife died I couldn't face the thought of another relationship. Dallas reckons I'm crazy, says I should shut up about Hannah and get on with life. I ignore him, of course. He isn't exactly the best role model. But then this wonderful woman enters my life and says she wants the kind of life I've been avoiding."

"I see. Two very different people, wanting different things from life. Sounds like you've had a narrow escape."

"Yeah. But..."

There was a long pause and Lucia couldn't stand the tension anymore. She didn't want to go through all this again. She didn't think she could stand it. "Nice to see you again, Guy, but I think it's time for me to leave."

He reached out and placed his hand on her arm. "Wait, please, Lucia. You know the woman is you. I'm sorry I hurt you."

She shouldn't have felt so much from the brief apology, but she couldn't help herself. Hope was like that. No matter how much she knew by experience that nothing could come from something, hope refused to die. "Thank you," she said softly.

"You're welcome."

She cleared her throat. It was only an apology—no doubt to make him feel better. "I've been meaning to contact you, actually. I'm making progress with your painting. I've received a report from an overseas expert which you should look at."

"Hope this isn't costing you too much time and money?"

"No. It's my job. And it's also my interest. I can't bear to think something is genuine and unacknowledged."

"Really? You know, I don't think it matters too much to me."

"Maybe. But I need to know."

She'd forgotten how blue his eyes were. A bright, bright blue that was a contrast to his dark hair and tanned skin. And their shape. Not large, but narrow and completely sexy. Even in repose, he looked at you as if he were imagining you with no clothes on and what he'd do to you. It made her *feel* naked and turned her mind to what things she could do to him. Ridiculous! She shouldn't be thinking about such things, not if she wanted to keep up her guard.

"I thought so. I don't know you well, but I do know that you can't walk away from something unfinished."

Her guard slipped another notch. "Sounds like you know me better than I know you."

"We can remedy that. How about dinner. Now?"

She really shouldn't. She felt herself nodding in agreement. "That would be nice. We could talk about your painting."

"We could." But the tweak at the corners of his mouth and sparkle in his eyes made it likely that he had little intention of spending much time on that particular subject. He nodded. "Good. After all, we have to work together over the coming weeks. We need to get on."

Her smile froze on her face. She felt its brief bloom fade and die on her lips. He was being pragmatic, of course. He simply wanted to clear the air to enable them to work together.

"Dinner then?" he continued. "How about Clark's?" While the waterfront restaurant was exclusive, it was most often used for business meetings and had no ambiance to speak of.

"Sure." She could only manage one word before she gestured toward the cloakroom and smiled.

"You go and get your things, and I'll meet you out front."

She felt his eyes on her as she walked away.

After all, he was only sorry he hurt her. Not for wanting a future he still obviously saw as very different to hers.

———

The city lights spread all around them, reflected on the inky black harbor. Across the water the lights of a plane flashed amber as it ascended rapidly away from the airport. The exclusive restaurant was busy with corporate types, and politicians, winding down before catching the late night flights back to their constituencies. But Guy had eyes for no one other than the beautiful woman before him.

Keep it cool, Guy repeated to himself. It was obvious that Lucia wasn't interested in what he could offer. So he'd chosen a neutral restaurant, one that wouldn't have her run a mile. But it was equally obvious that keeping cool was the last thing he could do. He didn't know how he'd been able to keep away from her these past months.

But, thanks to Dallas, he had the chance to at least be in her company once more. He'd take what he could get for the moment.

He sat back in his chair and looked across at Lucia as she spoke animatedly about the art. He half-listened, but the other half couldn't believe he'd put up with all those weeks away from her. How could he have been such a fool?

He smiled in response to her smile, but it wasn't what she was saying that got him. It was the way the flame from the candle shone in her eyes, bright with enthusiasm for her subject. He sighed and tilted his head to one side as she looked out across the dark harbor, talking about some abstract concept, her dark hair straight and shining under the subdued light. It was as if the light came from her, rather than she reflected it back—a light that had been missing from his life and that he'd had no idea about until that light had turned its beam to him. He supposed that you didn't know you moved in darkness until you saw the light. And then you couldn't imagine being without it.

"So do you get Shane Cotton's vision now?" she said, sitting back and swirling her wine in the glass, before putting it on the table, untouched.

"Nope. But I'm glad you do, for Shane's sake."

She laughed. "I don't think Shane Cotton will mind either way. He's doing his thing—"

"And people are paying hundreds of thousands for it. Good on him." He leaned forward. "But, you know, I'd rather talk about something else."

Lucia looked briefly uncomfortable, and he frowned. You couldn't tell with Lucia what she was thinking. If *he* was an open book, *she* was totally unreadable. Maybe that was part of her attraction.

"About your painting?" She reached for her phone. "I have the email here, with the report if you'd like to see it. It's quite technical."

"No, leave it for now."

"I think we should talk about it. It's pretty clear from what my colleague says that he believes my analysis is correct. There are very few people who can authenticate it. It seems I'm one of the few."

"Who are the others?"

She shrugged.

"It's only you, isn't it?"

She nodded.

He sat back in his chair. "So, what do I do if it's genuine? Keep it quiet? Or try to discover the whereabouts of the person who believes they bought the original from us?"

"I know who the person is."

"How? When we tried to research it at the original sale, we came up with a blank."

Lucia didn't shift her direct gaze, but it didn't help—she was still unreadable. "I just know. He's a Chinese businessman."

"But how?"

Another pause. "My mother made inquiries for me."

"That's good of her. So what next?"

"I'm waiting to hear from her. She wanted to check a few things."

"What did you tell her?"

"That you want the original verified."

"If it is, that would make his a fake. He's not going to be too happy about that."

"Indeed. That's where my mother comes in. She believes it's only a matter of time before the news leaks out about the painting. She believes it's best to address the matter. She's offered to contact him to resolve things, after discussing it with you, that is."

"Are you sure she doesn't mind doing this?"

"I'm sure. There's no need to worry about my mother. She can handle herself."

"Sounds a force to be reckoned with."

"Oh yes."

"Okay then. But before she contacts him, I'll take legal advice on whether we can dispute the original sale and keep the painting. It was sold for a fraction of its worth, on the understanding it would be kept in the Museum of New Zealand."

"It's a shame if it has to be returned. I almost wish I'd been wrong. You could have continued to enjoy it."

He shrugged. "It's best to know the truth. That way it can be cared for properly. But maybe we can delay the moment for a while. There's no hurry. We'll see what my lawyers advise. Anyway, that's enough about the painting. I want to thank you for accepting my apology and coming to dinner."

She shrugged again. "As you said, Dallas has made it impossible for us to ignore each other, so it's in everyone's interests that we get on."

"It's more than that, Lucia. You *know* it is."

"We want different things. That's what you said and you were right."

"That's what I thought. But I've amended that. A bit. Dallas made me re-think. And, I know, up to a point, he's right."

"And *I* know that you don't want a future with me. You

made that very clear."

He sighed tensely. "I'm saying, *really* badly, that while marriage and family aren't on my immediate radar, they are something I *do* want. Eventually. I'm saying that maybe we're not so different from each other after all. I'm saying... no, I'm *asking* if you'll give me another chance."

The sounds of the other diners faded away and all Guy was conscious of was Lucia's prolonged silence. Her beautiful face was as still as ever but her eyes looked down, and he suddenly realized that that was what she did whenever she was confused, whenever she thought her eyes might betray her true thoughts and feelings.

"Look at me, Lucia, and tell me what you're thinking." He reached over and tilted her chin. "Please."

She could have resisted his touch, it was too gentle to force her to face him, but she didn't. And in that gaze he saw the confusion and immediately felt hope.

"I'm sorry, Guy, but I can't jump into a relationship that's going nowhere, no matter how I feel. I can't wait around for 'eventually' to come round. We're two very different people, from two very different worlds. I can't see a future for us."

He sat back and nodded, disappointed. But what had he expected? This was Lucia—a woman who knew what she wanted, and what she didn't want. There was no way she could be wooed by a few honeyed words.

"I understand." He raised his hand for the check. "That's cool. I'll walk you home."

It was only a five minute walk across the quay to Lucia's apartment building, but it was long enough for Guy to realize that he wasn't going to give up on Lucia. He'd prove to her that he was a risk worth taking. And Dallas had given him the chance to do just that.

CHAPTER FIVE

L ucia joined in the applause at the end of Rachel's cooking demonstration. This time there were no TV cameras, no helpers, and not a celebrity in sight. Only a classroom packed full of teenage moms and their babies and toddlers. But the applause and chatter were louder and warmer than usual.

Apparently, Rachel had been supporting the school for teenage moms for years. And the moms of *He Huarahi Tamariki*—A Chance for Children—loved her.

Rachel was at the center of a crowd of young women, and she beckoned Lucia over to join her.

"This is my best friend Lucia, everyone."

"Hey, Lucia!" the girls called out. Some high-fived and others, whom she'd never met, gave her a hug. Lucia had been taken aback by the hugging which had greeted them both upon entering, and still hadn't got used to it. She smiled, unsure, and took a step away, hoping no one would notice her discomfort. But Rachel did.

"Hey, Tui, why don't you show Lucia your gorgeous little girl?"

Tui didn't need asking twice and proudly pushed a bundle of soft pink blankets toward Lucia. She grinned and pulled back a blanket to reveal a sleeping baby who couldn't have been more than six weeks old.

"She's beautiful," said Lucia, gently stroking the baby's downy head. She swallowed the lump and looked into Tui's dark, happy eyes. The girl couldn't have been more than sixteen and she looked like she hadn't a care in the world. "Does she sleep well?"

"She does now, since I've started back at school. Before that, it was difficult what with all the family, my aunty and uncle, and their *whanau* around all the time. But now things are good." She beamed again.

Lucia nodded, remembering that *whanau* was Maori for family. "Sounds like you've plenty of support at home."

The girl's face fell a little. "Plenty of people around, don't know about support though. I feel alone much of the time. I guess that's why I always wanted my own baby. She loves me and wants me, and only me, all the time." Tui cradled the baby closer to her chest.

Lucia felt an echo of the girl's loneliness stir within her own heart and didn't answer, scared her voice would break with emotion.

Tui looked up at Lucia suddenly. "I guess someone like you doesn't know what that's like. To want to be loved. To feel alone."

Lucia pressed her lips together and shook her head. "You guess wrong." That hole in her heart widened and she felt it like a gaping wound, directing every move, selecting every decision, every choice she made. She was like Tui, wanting a baby not for its own sake, but for a lack she felt within herself. She swiped away her tears.

Tui bent low. "What's up, miss? You got something in your eye?"

Lucia didn't look up, simply nodded. "A bit of hay fever I think. Anyhow, don't think you're alone in feeling lonely. There are plenty like us."

"Wow, miss. I know heaps of men who'd be happy to make you less lonely!" She grinned.

Lucia laughed. "Thanks, but no thanks! I'm steering clear of men for a while. All they bring is trouble."

"Don't I know it!" She stroked the baby's cheek and the baby turned her face automatically to suckle her finger. "Her father scarpered as soon as he knew I was pregnant."

Lucia's heart went out to the girl who'd found love in this tiny baby. She looked up at Rachel who was playing with another young woman's toddler. And her heart also went out to her friend, Rachel, who, for whatever reason, had backed the school for so long. It was people like her who'd given Tui a future.

Lucia swallowed down her tears and blinked. "It was lovely to meet you, Tui. I have to go now, but I'll return. I have some things which might come in useful."

"What sort of things?"

Lucia's tears were checked by Tui's obvious interest in whatever she could bring. She grinned.

"Clothes, toys."

"Choice, thanks." She gave Lucia a big, sunny smile. "See you around then."

As Rachel and Lucia drove into Wellington, Lucia focused on the view.

"You did that on purpose, didn't you, Rach?"

Rachel didn't answer immediately, but checked her rear-view mirror, signaled and overtook a car. "Did what on purpose?"

Lucia continued to watch the vista open out as they swept down the gorge and turned onto the motorway which hugged the bright blue harbor. "Took me there to show me why those young women had babies so young."

Rachel shrugged. "There are lots of reasons to have babies. Some are accidents, others are much wanted, despite their mother's young age."

"Lots of reasons," Lucia echoed. "And few of them the right one." She looked at Rachel for the first time, who met her gaze. "Especially mine."

The sun beat down on Wellington Zoo, trapping the heat in the sheltered valley, and Lucia wished she hadn't decided on looking professional over feeling comfortable. She wriggled her feet in her high sandals. Why hadn't anyone told her that the zoo was so hilly?

She listened to the zoo administrator as he explained at great lengths about the new education building they'd open if they received money from the trust. He didn't realize it was a done deal. She and Guy had already decided on that, even before they'd arrived at the zoo. It seemed Guy held very fond memories of the place and wanted to see it flourish. She'd almost wished they'd signed and sealed the deal without the tour. It was so damned hot.

She glanced at Guy who looked totally at ease and cool, with his open-necked white shirt and sunglasses. His hair was slightly longer than when she'd first met him and was pushed back from his face. It suited him, she thought. It added a sensuousness to the strong lines of his jaw and cheekbones—although his lips needed no added sensuality. She suddenly had a flashback to what those lips could do to her and her temperature sky-rocketed again. She felt a little faint and grabbed the bench for support.

Guy frowned and turned to the zoo administrator. "Let's check out the café facilities next." He glanced at Lucia. "I know for a fact that my colleague loves ice cream."

Lucia raised an eyebrow in query which he ignored.

"Certainly," replied the administrator. "Some of the funds will go to re-developing this area, as well. If we can attract people into the zoo with superior facilities, we hope they'll get behind our Kea Conservation Trust and Places for Penguins campaign."

They walked over to the small hut which served as the café. Lucia wrinkled her nose at the smell of fried chips that hung over the area. She hoped the new café would provide an alternative to greasy fried food.

She sat gratefully on a wooden bench in the shade, with an ice cream cone. She couldn't remember the last time she'd eaten a cone.

The administrator returned to his office, leaving them alone. Guy sat opposite, leaning against the stone wall, his arm along its length and watched her. She stopped licking.

"What?"

"Nothing," Guy said.

"If it's nothing why are you staring at me like that?"

"Because you're sitting opposite me. And... besides, you're providing the best view."

She looked around. On one side Wellington stretched out toward a shimmering sea. On the other, a couple of chimpanzees were putting on a show for the crowds. "Really?"

"Yes." He moved forward and placed his folded arms on the table between them. His gaze ranged over her face. "Even though you don't look one hundred percent well."

She shrugged. "Just hot."

He glanced at her ice cream. "Indeed. And if you don't eat that fast, you'll be wearing it."

She looked as a big blob of ice cream began to trickle down the cone. She licked it and then twisted the cone and pushed her hair to one side, and set to cleaning the cone. Then she made a mistake. She stopped licking and looked at him.

He pushed up his sunglasses and she could see pure, unadulterated lust. It offset the coolness of the ice cream. She didn't even notice the ice cream trickle onto her hand until he reached over and ran his finger along her fingers, scooping up the escaping ice cream and licking it.

She felt as though he were licking her. And it was her turn to melt at the thought.

He sat back and replaced his sunglasses. "So what do you think?"

Her heart was racing. Was he suggesting they return to her apartment? Was he thinking the same as her? "I think... we ought to wait. We shouldn't rush this. But..." She looked into his eyes and all thought of waiting fled. "But maybe I'm wrong."

He frowned. "I thought we'd agreed before we came here. The proposal's good. This is just a rubber-stamping."

She took a sharp intake of breath. "Yes... yes, er..." She trailed off, going over in her mind what she'd just said to him, hoping he hadn't understood her true meaning.

"The accommodation does need updating." He pointed to a building nestled in the trees, just outside the zoo fence. "You see that building? I remember having a sleepover there one night with my class."

If he had understood where her thoughts were going, he wasn't letting on. Thank goodness! "A sleepover?"

"Yeah. We were woken at dawn by the gibbons and lions. My mother came along as teacher's help."

"How old were you?" She took another mouthful of ice cream.

"Oh, about twenty."

She nearly spluttered out her ice cream. She swallowed and laughed. The release of tension felt good.

"I'm kidding. I was probably around nine or ten. It was pretty cool. Although I don't think Mum thought it was so cool, being kept awake all night by giggling kids, woken at dawn by screeching animals, and then dealing with over-tired children the next day."

"Sounds like fun."

"Maybe for people who like kids, but that person wasn't my mother. Her idea of fun doesn't include taking kids to the toilet in the middle of the night, or sleeping on the floor in a sleeping bag."

"Wasn't she expecting that?"

"I somehow forgot to tell her."

"I bet she enjoyed it in the end."

"In hindsight, maybe. It's provided her with a few jokes at my expense."

"I'd like to hear them."

"Really? You'd like to see my parents again?"

Lucia shrugged. "I simply meant I'd love to hear the stories."

"Right."

They sat awkwardly looking at each other for a few moments. Then Guy leaned toward her and Lucia's heart stopped. Before she could say anything, he finished off most of the remaining ice cream with one mouthful.

"Hey! You said you didn't want one."

"I didn't, because I knew I'd be having half of yours.

Come on." He rose and extended a hand to her. "Let's finish our tour."

They walked toward the entrance and offices. Cicadas throbbed loudly and heat shimmered on the concrete paths. Lucia suddenly felt strange and stopped walking.

"Are you okay?"

She felt her forehead with the back of her hand. "Just warm. Wow, it's hotter than I thought."

Guy frowned. "You do look flushed. How about we finish here—put them out of their misery and tell them we'll recommend the board approves their application—and go on to our next call out near the airport? It'll be cooler."

"Sounds good."

Guy was right. After they'd completed their next appointment in air-conditioned offices, Lucia felt much better. As they drove past the end of the airport runway, a plane flew low overhead.

"Wow! That was close."

Guy slowed and watched the plane bank and turn to head away from Wellington. "Would you believe I'd never left New Zealand until my late teens?" He looked around, up at the hills and his expression became thoughtful. "I loved it here. And couldn't think of any reason to leave. When my parents went overseas on vacation, I insisted they leave me with my friends."

He looked out toward the road that hugged the shoreline beyond the airport, which led to the rocky point that overlooked the harbor entrance. "My mother's family lived on this land for generations. Right from the days of the earliest settlers."

"Really? You must feel a real connection with the place. Shame you have to travel for work so much."

He pressed his lips together. "Oh, I've moved on from those days. New Zealand will always be my home, but now I prefer to keep moving. And I would be, if Dad hadn't wanted me in New Zealand to look after the family's businesses. It has got too much for him to handle, so he's focusing on the winery now."

The reminder that their wishes were so far apart made Lucia look away. Why the hell did Dallas keep pushing them together when it was obvious that Guy no more wanted to stay in one place than to have children?

She shifted in her seat and pushed away her hair from her face and looked toward the hills where Guy's family had once settled, and felt once more the depths of Guy's grief over the loss of his wife. He'd obviously loved her so much—with a love that he had no wish to find again—that he couldn't bear to stay in the places which reminded him of her.

"Would you like to see the place where my forebears lived?"

She was surprised. "Yes, I'd love to."

They drove past the airport and along the narrow road which wound around the headland, before pulling into a small carpark. "It's here."

"Here?" She looked up at the overgrown gully and steep slope over which brambles and gorse grew. "What's here?"

He slammed the car door closed. "It's a steep path. Are you up to it?"

She peered upward dubiously. "Sure."

"It's not too far."

They walked to the top where there was a World War I memorial commemorating Ataturk, the Turkish commander. They neared it and read the inscription of Ataturk's famous speech.

"'You, the mothers'"—read Lucia—"'who sent their sons from faraway countries wipe away your tears; your sons are now lying in our bosom and are in peace. After having lost their lives on this land, they have become our sons as well.'" Lucia was moved. "Oh!" The word was wrenched out of her and tears sprung to her eyes at the thought of the men—barely out of childhood—who were buried in a faraway country—men younger than her brother had been when he'd died.

"Yes, I know," said Guy. "Apparently they built the memorial here because it was similar to the place they renamed Anzac Cove in Turkey where so many Australian and New Zealand Army Corps soldiers lost their lives."

The rocky promontory faced the opposite shore where a lighthouse stood. Between the two was a narrow strait—the only way in or out of Wellington harbor. Inside the harbor, the sea was smooth, outside, choppy.

"In winter, the sea rages outside the harbor. My mother's family used to live here. My great, great—I can't remember how many greats—grandfather, was Wellington's pilot, bringing ships safely into harbor. The local Maori who lived at the edge of the gully used to row him out to incoming ships when they received the signal from Mt Albert, where the first signal station was sited."

Looking at the sea churning around the dangerous rocks even on a calm day, Lucia couldn't imagine it. "He must have been brave."

"And his family was, too. Picture it. A mud-clad house, tucked just in the lee of the hill, overlooking the gully. Pretty wild."

Lucia shivered. It was a long way from anywhere she'd

been brought up—her Italian grandmother's house, her boarding school in the UK and latterly, the towers of Shanghai. "It must have been very lonely."

"They had company. My great, great, whatever, aunts apparently used to ride their horses over to the neighboring bay, where the airport is now. And the family was big. Too big for a small two-bedroomed cottage."

"So both sides of your family have been in Wellington since it was first settled?"

"Pretty much. My father's family was one of the first pioneers to travel over the Wai Drop as they used to call it to Wairarapa and settle in Onihau. They couldn't believe their luck after this terrain. Over there they had space to grow crops. Here? There was little they could do with any of this."

His eyes narrowed against the bright light as he turned away from the hills above Wellington, which was all they could see from their vantage point, and back to look out to the tossing seas of the Strait which separated them from the South Island.

For a brief moment, she could almost believe he was his ancestor—the brave ship's pilot. And she felt envy for all that he had, all that she wanted, and all that he was determined to turn his back against. Tanned by the sun, his shirt flapping in the swift breeze, he looked upon the land with a sense of ownership that only long association could bring. He belonged here as surely as she belonged nowhere. Only why couldn't he see it?

"Can you see the Kaikouras?" Guy continued. "They're the mountains that run down the east coast of the South Island."

Reluctantly she tore her gaze from him and looked across the waters to the misty horizon above which a range of snow-capped mountains floated. "They look unreal."

"They're real enough." She looked at him and his gaze now rested on her. Her hair lifted and spun around her head, but she didn't try to stop it. She felt different up here. And he looked different, as if he'd forgotten his need to be free of this land. There was just him and her, their past and futures forgotten. He took her hand. "They're real enough," he repeated. "As real as anything else around here." He squeezed her hand. "As real as you and me."

She shook her head. "No." She pointed to the hill, beyond which lay the city. "That's where we're real. Not here. Not now."

He reached over and brushed away her hair, which was swirling around her face, and rested his palm against her cheek, his thumb stroking her skin. "Maybe we should stay here then."

"You don't want to be real?"

"No. Because up here I feel anything's possible."

"No, no it's not."

He narrowed his eyes. "I could do what I've wanted to do all day, up here."

"What's that?" she breathed.

"I could kiss you."

She shook her head against his hand. "That's not a good idea."

"Then why is your pulse hammering under my fingers? Why do I read an entirely different message in your eyes, and why"—he brushed his thumb against her lips—"have you moved your face closer to mine?"

She couldn't breathe, couldn't think under the devastating effect of his fingers against her face, his breath on her cheek and his mouth so close to hers. Then he brushed his lips against hers, and she felt his sharp intake of breath as he kept them there, gently pressed against hers, just for a moment before, too soon, he pulled away.

He stepped back, pushed his hands through his hair in confusion and cursed. His regret was obvious and cut her to the bone.

She suppressed the hurt and pulled her hair tight in a twist and looped it into a knot. "I think it's time we were going. We still have that paperwork to complete."

"Sure, sure." He couldn't even look her in the eye. She walked toward the path and continued down, not pausing to see if he followed. She picked up her pace, needing to put space between them, angry with both him and herself for allowing it to happen. There was no point—absolutely no point in beginning anything that could go nowhere.

He'd clicked open the car door for her, and she got in ahead of him. As they drove off, she took one last look at the place that connected him so securely to this country and turned away. The fact that he didn't want that and she did, made her feel the divide between them more keenly still.

———

The drive to Lucia's apartment was a quiet one. Guy glanced at Lucia. She was looking across the bays, away from him. It was obvious that she didn't want anything from him. It was bad enough in the zoo, when he'd nearly forgotten himself and kissed her. Thank God he recovered so she hadn't realized. But up there, on the bluff? Something had got to him, something he hadn't felt in a long time. For a brief moment, the feelings of guilt which had consumed him since Hannah's death had left him, and he'd felt free. And there was only one thing he wanted... Lucia.

And he hadn't been able to contain his desire for her, to touch her, to kiss her. And she hadn't been able to hide the fact that, no matter her intentions, she desired him. But she wasn't giving in to them, and she couldn't get out of there and back into the car quick enough.

He turned into the underground garage of her apartment, the wheels squealing on the concrete floor as he took the corner faster than he should, and pulled up sharp. Lucia jerked forward a little with the abrupt halt. He couldn't help it. It was as if he wanted to see her react—any reaction —so he could gauge her thoughts. But when he turned to her she had her head averted, as she gathered her things.

"Would you like to come in?" she asked.

Maybe he was wrong. Maybe she did want to have a more personal relationship. "Sure."

It wasn't until they'd entered her apartment that he realized why. "I'll find the papers Dallas sent over. We can sign and approve those applications and get them out of the way."

"Of course." He reached over and pressed the button on the elevator. "That just leaves the Tanakina application."

"The school for troubled kids?"

"Yes Dallas thinks we should visit the school to see exactly how they intend to use the funds. Their application is for a large sum."

"Hm, I guess he's right. Where is the school exactly?"

The elevator doors slid open revealing the lobby to her apartment. Guy followed Lucia but stopped suddenly. "What's my painting doing here?"

"It's not yours. Yours is safe in the art gallery. I went and bought a print of it for you. See here, the printer's mark is on it. Thought I'd surprise you. I felt guilty."

"Guilty? Why?" He inspected the print.

"Because, I've effectively robbed you of something you loved."

"That depends on what my lawyer says. But I should imagine you're right. Despite my family's connection with the painting, and the circumstances around its initial sale, I've a feeling we'll have to return it. But I'm not in any rush."

"Well, when you do, you'll have this one in Onihau instead."

He grabbed her hand. "You, Lucia Rossi, are a wonderful woman." He wished he could have reclaimed the words which had poured out so thoughtlessly, so unconsidered, and so much from his heart, when he saw the look of confusion on her face. He let her hand slip from his.

"A simple 'thank you' would have done," she said quietly, her expression revealing a strange mixture of hurt, confusion and wistfulness, before she turned away. "The papers are in the living room, I think."

He watched as she walked to the desk set before a window overlooking the harbor. As she riffled through the papers, slightly bent over, her stream of dark hair highlighted by a slant of sunlight, the slightness of her hips accentuated by the figure-hugging dress she wore, he realized that what he'd said was heartfelt. She *was* a wonderful woman. But she was more to him than just that.

"Lucia... I—"

"Ah, here they are!" She swung around and held them out to him, just as the phone rang. "If you want to sort out the paperwork, I'll answer that."

Guy sighed and went over the papers. He couldn't seem to get through to her. Whenever he tried to speak, whenever he spoke from the heart, he stumbled. Trouble was, he didn't know why she was avoiding hearing what he had to say. Was it because she felt the same but for some reason didn't want to admit it, or was it simply because she felt nothing?

He sat, skim-read a contract and signed it. He could hear Lucia talking on the phone. He examined another document and frowned. They needed to discuss this application further. He couldn't hear Lucia talking and so picked up the contract and walked toward a small sitting room which she used as a media room. He could hear a voice, but it wasn't Lucia's. The door was only partially closed, so he pushed it open. The large computer screen which was fixed to the wall showed a woman, Lucia. What the—?

Then the woman spoke and he realized it must be her mother on a Skype call with Lucia. They looked so alike it was impossible it could be anyone else. He went to step away but was arrested by the mention of one word. "The Goldie—"

He stopped still.

"I've confirmed the owner of the painting," Lucia's mother continued.

"Who is it?" asked Lucia.

Her mother sighed and shook her head. "It's not good news, I'm afraid. I wondered when we couldn't find any trace of the owners through conventional means."

"The name?"

"Will mean little to you. The identity of the person is buried behind layers of fake companies. He's not generally known. His name is Zhang." Lucia's mother looked upward from where she'd previously been focused on Lucia and frowned. "Lucia! Who is that behind you?"

Guy stepped forward as Lucia swung around. "I'm Guy Martin, Mrs. Rossi. Pleased to meet you." He smiled. When caught eavesdropping, go on a charm offensive. "You look exactly like your daughter."

She gave a slight, guarded smile, Lucia's smile. "We do look alike, but maybe not exactly."

"Guy, sorry. My mother rang with some news." Lucia turned to her mother on the screen. "Yes, this is Guy, who owns the painting."

"It's a beautiful painting, but the fact you possess the original has made things... complicated, shall we say. But I have a few ideas on what to do about the situation."

"That would be great. I'm talking with my lawyers but it's a tricky situation."

"Maybe we can discuss my ideas another time." Lucia's mother turned her gaze back to Lucia and, from the look on both their faces, Guy couldn't help wondering if he would be party to the discussions, despite the fact it was his painting.

"Sure, Mother," Lucia said quickly.

Guy looked from one to the other and knew that they were hiding something from him. And he also knew that Lucia and her mother had developed the ability to hide things from the world—including themselves—to an art form.

"I hope we can meet again, Guy," said Lucia's mother.

"You must come to New Zealand, and we can show you around." He looked quickly at Lucia, suddenly realizing he'd used the plural pronoun. But she didn't say anything.

"That would be... interesting. Thank you. Until next time." She smiled, and her image vanished as she ended the call.

Lucia flicked on the lights and turned to him as if nothing had happened. "Coffee? And then we can finalize those papers."

Guy followed Lucia into the kitchen as she moved quickly around, heating up the coffee machine and producing some snacks.

"Lucia. What the hell is going on? Why was your mother so mysterious?"

She turned to him and folded her arms across her waist. "My mother knows people."

"*I* know people. *You* know people. I guess what you're saying is that your mother has—"

"Contacts. Exactly."

"So what does your mother plan to do?"

"I don't know yet. She'll tell me when we speak next, I expect."

"When I'm not here, obviously. Anyway, why should she plan to do anything? I'm still checking out our legal position."

"Because I asked her to."

"I want to make this clear. This is my painting. If there's a problem, then it's also mine, and I'll deal with it. Okay?"

"Sure." She bit her lip. "It's just that my mother knows this world."

"And what world might that be?"

Lucia hesitated. And, remembering Dallas's disclosure about her brother's gang affiliations, Guy knew why.

"Do you remember me telling you my brother kept bad company?" she continued.

"Yes."

"Well, he was in a gang."

"I see." Lucia paused and suddenly Guy really did see— too clearly. He groaned. "Don't tell me your mother is, too?"

She hesitated. "Her father—my grandfather—was. She still has contacts within the organization. She still has... respect."

"When you say organization, you mean the Chinese Triads, don't you?"

She bit her lip and nodded.

"And what you're also saying is that she knows how to deal with the situation better than me."

"You've got the idea." She passed him a cup of coffee, but didn't meet his gaze.

He might have the idea, but he doubted he knew a fraction of the full situation. As he drank his coffee and watched Lucia move quickly around the kitchen he wondered what the hell he was getting himself into.

CHAPTER SIX

The small plane landed on the narrow strip at the small airport and taxied bumpily toward the terminal building.

Lucia looked around at the golden hills of Marlborough, only their lower slopes visible under an unusual band of misty clouds. She glanced at the scattering of buildings they were approaching. "I don't think I've ever been to such a small airport."

"Me neither. I usually sail into the Sounds."

"I've never been here at all before." She looked around. "I'm not sure why Dallas insisted on us both coming. Seems a bit unnecessary to check out an adventure school for troubled children."

"Hm," Guy said ambiguously. "I'm not sure either, although I can guess."

So Guy thought the same as her. Dallas was determined to match them and was making sure he created enough opportunities for that to happen. "He's not letting up, is he?"

The flight attendant opened the door and they walked

down the steps and out across the tarmac that was gray under the lowering sky. "Doesn't look like it. But I think you're going to enjoy Tanakina. The drive takes us along the Queen Charlotte Sound which is stunning."

Guy was only partly right. The views were spectacular—wide expanses of the sound with only a scattering of houses along the way. But the road was also very winding, and Lucia felt quite queasy by the time they reached Tanakina. But that soon passed and the hours they spent at Tanakina camp sped by with equal ease. The camp was well run and inspirational. Lucia got to speak with camp leaders and students alike, learning about their diverse backgrounds, which she could relate to—even if hers had been a lot wealthier. And Guy was in his element—forgetting his hang-ups and playing rugby with a group of boys. He emerged from the game, beaming.

"I don't know who enjoyed that most—you or the boys!" laughed Lucia.

Guy grinned and slung his jacket over his shoulder. "Or you, perhaps? You look a different person."

"I feel a different person." She looked around her. "I wish I could stay here forever."

He was silent for a few moments. "I can't do forever, but I can do a night. My family's holiday home is only half an hour's boat ride away. It's empty. If you like, we could borrow a boat and go there for the night? There are plenty of bedrooms," he added hastily.

"I don't have anything with me."

"We keep essential supplies there. There'll be a change of clothes of my mother's you can use. You're roughly the same size. Although I can't guarantee your taste in clothes is the same." He grinned. "Would you like to go there?"

His grin did the usual heart-stopping thing, and not only stopping her heart, but also stopping her sense of self-preservation. "I'd love to."

After Guy did a quick shop at the Tanakina grocery store, they borrowed a small motor boat from the camp, and they were on their way.

She thought of the package she'd bought at Wellington airport on a whim, and had thrust to the bottom of her bag. It wasn't the first time she'd thought she should buy the kit. But each time the thought had teased her she'd swept it away. Simply wishful thinking. Nothing more.

Until now. This queasiness wouldn't go away. What if? No, Lucia placed the thought firmly to the back of her mind. It was impossible. She was simply logically elimi-nating possibilities. But, what if? The thought persisted, and Lucia frowned pensively at the rapidly graying sky.

"Don't worry about the rain. It looks like it'll keep off until we get there."

She looked up with surprise. She'd been so lost in her own thoughts, she hadn't noticed the overcast skies.

"You're not worried about the rain, are you? What's the matter?"

She shook her head without turning to him. "Just thinking of something."

"Anything I can help you with?"

"No. I'm fine."

He sighed. "You keep too many things hidden from the

world, Lucia. Hidden from me. It makes it hard..." He pressed his lips together as if he'd said too much.

"Hard to communicate?"

"Something like that." He was silent as he looked around and changed direction. "Here we are. We're entering the inlet where our house is now."

Guy turned the boat into a small inlet, and immediately the atmosphere changed. There were no houses on the steeply wooded hillsides, no sound of people, no boats, chainsaws, nothing but a brooding sense of mystery.

"So many native trees. It's amazing."

"There used to be forest all over Marlborough, but it was cleared for farming. Now all we have is small pockets of unspoiled land like this."

A dolphin suddenly leaped into the water in front of them, followed by others. Guy laughed. "It's a taniwha, guiding us home."

"Taniwha?"

"Maori tradition has it that a taniwha called Tuhirangi guided their ancestor into the Sounds. It was probably a dolphin. We get a lot of them round here."

Lucia leaned over to see better, letting her hand trail through the cool, clear water. She laughed. "I feel I could reach over and touch them."

"You can swim with them if you like."

"I'd very *much* like." She looked at him, standing at the prow of the boat, guiding them in, and thought about his Maori heritage. He looked Maori—with his dark hued skin —and she wondered whether he *felt* Maori. "So, did your great-great-grandmother being Maori influence how you were raised?"

"My grandmother made sure it did. She used to take me to the local marae to hang out with my extended family."

"And yet you don't go there often."

He was silent, scanning the wooded slopes, for what she didn't know. If it was answers, it didn't seem to help him any. He shrugged.

"I guess one doesn't always want to be with one's family," Lucia continued. "Look at me."

And he did. "Two outcasts together," he said. "Maybe we were made for each other."

"Maybe."

His light-hearted tone should have lessened the impact of what he'd said. She turned away from his gaze so he couldn't see the effect his words had on her. When she glanced at him, he was concentrating on steering the boat.

He drove the boat slowly, ensuring the boat's wake did minimal damage to the pristine banks, past small coves with sandy beaches above which was thick bush. There didn't appear to be any signs of habitation—only wildlife. Kingfishers flicked their tails and dove into the water, tuis warbled their two-tone songs and the melodic notes of a bellbird sang across the water, echoing as the hills around the sound grew closer in. The boat passed a rocky promontory and Lucia could suddenly see where they were headed.

Snuggled into the side of a bush-clad hill, the house—all wood and glass—revealed itself before them. Guy flicked through his key ring, pressed a small remote control and out from behind a screen of draping green climbers, a door whirred open. He cut the engine as they cruised up to, and through the open doors. Guy jumped out, tied up the boat and then helped Lucia onto the wooden jetty. The water slapped at the far end of the boathouse, and it smelled of wet vegetation.

Guy looked around, breathing in the earthy smells. "I

love this place. Whenever I come here I can't believe I've stayed away so long."

"Don't you feel the same about Onihau?"

He didn't speak immediately. "I used to."

"But?"

"Not so much now."

Lucia looked away. He never wanted to discuss his feelings about Onihau and she knew why. Because he was reminded of the wife he obviously hadn't got over.

"Anyway, let's go up to the house." He opened the door at the rear, which revealed wooden steps leading to the house. "Here's the key. Go on up and I'll follow with the supplies."

As Lucia climbed the steep steps she was aware of bird song filling the air. She did a 360-degree turn, absorbing the sound, smell and sight of it all. Rata vines hung from towering totara trees, and ferns of every size and description grew all around. With the mist beginning to form a soft rain, everything was a soothing, magical green.

The stairs emerged onto a deck that ran the length of a glass-lined facade overlooking the whole of the sound. Bush, raw and untampered with, layered the sides of the sound, lending its dark green reflection to the water—deep, cool and bottomless.

There was no other sign of habitation, nothing but birds, dolphins jumping at the sound's entrance, and the rustling of leaves.

Guy walked behind her. "What do you think?"

"It's wonderful. I feel like a bird must feel, perched in the trees."

"*That*, I believe, was the intention."

"I feel like I could take flight, soar over the water, over the trees, and into the open sky."

"You'll be flying away soon enough. In the meantime, perhaps you'd unlock the door?"

She turned to see Guy heavily laden. "Sorry!"

She unlocked the door and stood aside for Guy. She followed him in and paused, taking in the stylish but simple interior. A 1950s style open-plan space greeted her, with retro furnishings which complemented both the house and its setting. Nothing ostentatious, but with a solid, timeless beauty.

"Wow, this is amazing. I didn't imagine anything like this." She trailed her hands across the spines of books which lined one wall and plucked one at random.

"My family doesn't do the Kiwi bach, so much as a New York type loft, out in the bush. My grandmother wasn't interested in roughing it. It was she who insisted on the Mies van der Rohe chair."

Lucia turned to see the elegant chair positioned in front of the wall of glass. "I can imagine sitting there reading a book." She glanced at the title of the one in her hand. "Proust." She flipped it open. "In French."

"Yes, *Grandmère* was French. She was my mother's mother. Another nationality to add to the melting pot that is me. She was probably the last person who looked at half of those books."

"*À la Recherche du Temps Perdu*... In Search of Lost Time... or *Remembrance of Things Past* as it's better known."

"Your French accent is flawless. *Grandmère* would have approved."

"It should be. I majored in French and Art History at Shanghai University. I might be hard to communicate with in English, but I know my French."

He poured a glass of wine and handed her one. "*You* are a very surprising woman."

She shook her head about the wine. "Something soft? Sparkling water?"

"Sure." He poured her a glass. "Make yourself comfortable while I fix us some food."

"And you are full of surprises, too. I didn't know you could cook."

"I guess we don't know each other well, do we?" He raised his glass to hers. "Here's to getting to know each other better."

She raised her glass to his. "To finding out if we have anything else in common, other than that we're both misfits?" She grinned, and they clinked glasses.

"*Salut!*" He held her gaze, and she felt the heat rise, making her uncomfortable. She looked away.

"So... what are you cooking?"

He smiled as if he knew she was trying to break the connection between them. "Cooking? I think you can only use that term very loosely to describe what I'm about to do." He turned a package around in his hands and peered at the small print. "Five minutes in the microwave, I'm afraid. That's as far as my cooking goes tonight." He opened the microwave and slid the tray in.

The microwave hummed and Guy crossed his arms and looked at Lucia with a self-satisfied smile. "Tofu Spinach Ravioli will be ready in five minutes, ma'am."

She laughed. "Perfect." And it was. *He* was. Despite her better judgment she loved being with him. Watching him with the kids at Tanakina, she'd seen a different side to him. She felt she was watching the real Guy Martin, not the man whose grief had molded him into his present shape. No, the real Guy was a man who loved children and company and enjoyed belonging, both to people and to place. All the things she wanted. She smiled.

"What are you thinking?"

"That... you enjoyed being with the kids at the school today."

He placed some garlic bread in the oven. Lucia raised an eyebrow in surprise.

"What?" he said with mock indignation. He grinned. "It was all there was. Call it Italian-New Zealand fusion cooking."

"That just about covers everything."

"Yes, and about the kids, I did enjoy myself. It's good to be back in the Sounds."

"But didn't you come here with Hannah?"

"Only a couple of times. Why do you ask?"

She shrugged. "Because you don't seem to mind coming here, and you *really* mind being at Onihau."

"And why do you think that is?"

She turned and caught his serious gaze. "Sorry, it's none of my business."

"I think the line between our businesses is getting increasingly blurred. And, you know, it feels fine with me. So... tell me why you think I avoid Onihau."

"I'm sorry, Guy, I'm just guessing. I assumed it's to do with Hannah. I guess Onihau makes you think of what you've lost and what you'll never have again."

He'd folded his arms and leaned against the kitchen bench, his expression thoughtful. "You're right."

She turned away. She didn't want to be right.

"And wrong."

She smiled tightly and sat. "You're talking in riddles."

He came and sat opposite her. "You're right, being at Onihau, the place where I grew up, the place where I lived with Hannah after we married, is difficult for me now."

"So I was right."

"For the wrong reasons." He sighed. "Let me try to explain."

"You don't have to, not if you don't want to. I'm sorry, I didn't mean to pry."

"You're not. I *want* to tell you. Maybe if I say it aloud, I might get it straight in my mind. You see Hannah was killed in a car accident."

"I'm so sorry."

"I'm sorrier than most. It was my fault."

She looked at him and what she saw made her forget everything. She reached out and rested her hand on his arm. "You were driving?"

He closed his eyes briefly. "No. But... we'd had an argument which resulted in her returning home alone, late at night on icy roads." He paused again and swallowed. "She must still have been pretty angry because the cops reckoned she was traveling well over the speed limit."

"Oh my God!"

"She was killed outright. At least she didn't suffer." He cleared his throat and shifted slightly in his seat.

"You don't have to tell me this, not if it's upsetting."

"No, I want you to know. You see Hannah and I, we were best friends growing up. Wherever Hannah was, I'd be found. As we grew older we discovered sex, and our relationship changed to accommodate that. And we got married because that was what everyone expected of us. I never questioned it. We just"—he shrugged—"*went* together." He sighed and leaned forward, resting his arms on his legs. "Or so I thought. I remember waking up one morning, a few years into our marriage, and realizing that I'd made a terrible mistake. You see, I wasn't in love with her. Oh, I loved her as a friend. Just no more than that. But she'd given up the opportunity for a sports scholarship in the US to get married. And she resented it. She became more and more possessive as the years went by. It drove me crazy. She resented me doing things I enjoyed, like rugby. That night, the night she died, I'd had enough. We'd been married five years and by then she hated me playing rugby, hated seeing me with my mates and wanted me to stop. I refused. She left. And she died."

"Ah," said Lucia. "And I guess you haven't played rugby with your team since."

He pressed his lips together and shook his head. "Correct."

"Some kind of penance?"

He frowned. "Maybe. All I know is that if I'd gone with her, rather than stay at the rugby club, she'd still be alive today."

She caressed his arm, desperate to try to reassure him. "But it was her decision to leave. You can't be held responsible for somebody else's actions."

"I can. And I am." He shook his head and jumped up, pacing in front of the window. Outside, the trees and water were now cloaked in a veil of soft, gray rain. "Whenever I'm at Onihau I'm reminded of how I ruined that wonderful woman's life. Because she *was* a wonderful girl, who'd grown into a wonderful woman, one I should have walked away from. I should have insisted she follow her dreams of becoming a professional athlete. But I was this macho rugby-playing man who believed I should be at the center of a woman's world." He looked at Lucia with urgent eyes. "I no longer believe that. Far from it."

She wanted to ask him what he *did* believe in, whether

there was a slither of hope that she could grab that would take her into a future with him. She wanted to ask if they—Lucia and Guy—had any future at all. She sucked in a deep breath, and then the microwave went ding, and they both turned to look. When she looked at Guy, she realized the moment had passed.

He smiled briefly, but the shadows of sadness still lingered in his eyes.

Lucia had thought he was a straightforward man, a man unused to concealing pain. Seemed that most everyone was broken in some way or other. It made her open her heart a little more to him, which was the last thing she wanted.

It was dark by the time they'd finished eating. There were no lights to penetrate the misty black, nothing but the hoot of owls and the soft splash of the water on the bank below the deck. The vegetation was lush and draped over the edges of the house. The air was damp.

Guy joined Lucia on the deck under the shelter of the overhanging roof, and rested his arms on the rail, looking out into the mist. "You can see the full length of the sound when there's no mist. And, believe it or not, there usually isn't."

"It feels so unreal. Like we've stepped away from life, hidden from everyone and everything."

He turned to look at her, but she couldn't meet his eye. "And is that a good thing?"

She bit her lip as she considered her answer.

He rested his hand on her arm. "No, Lucia. Don't consider your answer. Tell me straight. What do you feel?

Do you mind being hidden away from everyone, with only me for company?"

Like droplets of mist, his words hung in the air, waiting for an answer. She shook her head and then looked at him. "No. No, I don't mind being hidden, with only you for company." She swallowed.

He reached out and gently ran his knuckles along her cheek and jaw. "Good. Because, right now, I couldn't think of anywhere I'd rather be." Before she could respond he'd bridged the slight distance between them and kissed her gently on the lips. He pulled away slightly, as if waiting to see her response. She put her hand around the nape of his neck, caressed it briefly before pulling him toward her.

This time, the kiss was long and slow, his lips were gentle and sensitive against hers, caressing more than demanding. But with each sweet brush of his lips against hers, each caress of his hand over her back, she wanted more. She deepened the kiss and was rewarded with a sharp intake of breath from Guy. She stepped closer, until her body was pressed hard against his. She wanted to feel every inch of him against her, in her. He took her hand, and in that moment she knew exactly what she wanted—to be with him. No matter what.

Lucia awoke early and slipped out of bed to the bathroom. She dug around in her handbag and produced the pregnancy kit she'd bought on impulse the day before. The doctors had told her that it would be near impossible to get pregnant without fertility treatment. And her periods hadn't stopped. They were lighter maybe, but hadn't stopped. But the continuing queasiness couldn't be attributed to a tummy bug any longer. No, she'd take the test just to put her mind at rest. She sat on the edge of the bath for some time waiting for it to show a result.

There were two solid lines, one less solid, but still there. She couldn't seem to think straight. Did that mean she was pregnant or not pregnant? She quickly scanned the instructions and looked at her shocked reflection in the mirror.

She *was* pregnant.

For the first time, she noticed that she had lost a little weight, her face looked less full. And her mind ran over all the times she'd been put off eating by the smell of food cooking, put off her favorite perfume, put off drinking alcohol. She pressed her forehead against the bathroom mirror, needing its coolness to seep into her hot mess of a brain.

Pregnant! But that was what she wanted, wasn't it?

She stepped away from the mirror and looked at herself again. Yes, it was what she wanted, but Guy had made it quite clear that he didn't want a long-term relationship soon, nor children. But seeing him with the kids yesterday, she knew, just knew, that he'd make a great father and family man. Surely he realized that too? Surely he'd be as thrilled as she was?

When Guy awoke, he looked for Lucia but she was gone. He gazed up at the sarked wood ceiling. The damp breeze from an open window played against his naked skin, but it did nothing to cool his desire. Making love to Lucia was a revelation. He thought he'd never feel anything again after Hannah had died. He'd *decided* never to feel anything again. But then Lucia had appeared, and he'd had no choice *but* to feel. He wanted her in his life, about that there was no doubt. And, so long as she knew he couldn't commit more than for the present only, then, just possibly, their relationship could work.

He walked out into the main room and saw her standing on the deck, silhouetted against the soft light of a new dawn. The mist was slowly clearing, revealing the dark green water, which mirrored the lush, primitive forest. Birds skimmed across the water, and the strident sounds of native birds echoed over the inlet. Suddenly the sun rose above the hills, flooding the inlet with light, making the dew on the trees glitter like diamonds and edging her silhouette with a brilliant light.

He felt a distance between them which he was desperate to bridge. He took a step toward her and she turned suddenly.

"Guy! How long have you been standing there?"

"Long enough to want you in my bed again."

She smiled. "You have a one-track mind, Mr. Martin."

He gave a rueful grin. "It's true. But perhaps if you come to bed with me now, I'll experiment, see if I can't develop a multi-track mind."

He suddenly realized there was something in her eyes which was different.

"What is it, Lucia? Are you okay?"

She nodded.

"Have you been awake long?"

"Long enough." He frowned, but before he could ask her what she meant, she continued. "Guy, yesterday at Tanakina, I could see how much you enjoyed being with the kids. Surely..."

"Surely what?"

She shrugged. "It's just I don't understand... why you

say you don't want children when it's obvious how much you enjoy them."

"Yes, I enjoyed being in their company. But I enjoy many things. It doesn't mean to say I want them *all* the time. I don't." He put his hands around her shoulders. "Lucia, last night made me realize I want to be with you but I stand by what I've said in the past. I can't commit to a future with you, with anyone. How do you feel about taking our relationship day by day? See how we go?"

Her face froze, and she shook her head jerkily. "No, I can't do 'day by day', Guy."

"Why not?"

"Because I have to look longer than that."

"How long?"

"At least six months."

"Why, what's happening in six months?"

"I'll be giving birth to our baby."

CHAPTER SEVEN

Guy retreated instantly—physically and emotionally. From the moment his hand fell from her shoulders, and he stepped away, she knew. She didn't even have to see the stunned look in his eyes to have her fears confirmed. He stood frozen for a moment, his back to her. "Pregnant?" he half-whispered to himself. "Pregnant?" he asked again louder this time.

"Yes. I'm sorry you seem to think this is bad news."

"Bad news?" He swung around to face her. "What the hell did you think? That I'd be thrilled? You know I don't want children."

"Yet." She stood taller and lifted her chin. "Yet," she said with emphasis. "You said you don't want children *yet*, but later..." She bit her lip, her courage failing her.

"Later isn't now."

"You made love to me, without condoms. You took the risk."

"Because you said you were infertile."

She winced at the word. She might use it, but she hated to hear it on the lips of others. "I was told I was." She sucked in a deep breath. "Apparently doctors don't know everything."

"Apparently." Guy pushed his fingers through his hair and paced away. He stayed there for a second before twisting around to look out into the mid-distance. But not at her. It seemed he had nothing to say to her. "What a mess!"

"No, it's not."

"In what way is this *not* a mess?"

"In the way that *you* don't have to do anything. I'll sort this out."

He looked up slowly at her for the first time since she's told him. "You'll do *what*?"

"I'll sort it out."

"You're not terminating the pregnancy."

She was shocked by his tone. "Is that a question or an order?"

"Both."

"No, I'm not. Of course, I'm not. Why would I do a thing like that when this is what I want, and thought I could never have? I'm surprised that you're not encouraging me to do exactly that. You've made it patently clear you don't want children."

"What I want, or don't want, is now irrelevant. The fact is you're pregnant, and I'm not in favor of termination."

"Me neither. My God, at last we've found something we have in common," she said facetiously.

"So what did you mean that you'll sort this out?"

"All I mean is that you don't have to be involved in any way."

He shook his head. "You think I'd walk away?"

"I've no idea what you'll do. But I'm giving you that option."

"Well, I don't wish to take it. There is no way in this world I'd ever walk away from a child of mine."

"Even though you don't want one."

"Exactly."

"It's a contradiction."

"It's a fact."

Lucia stood stock still, clenching her fists to keep a rein on her emotions, as Guy stood so close to her, hands on hips. She refused to back away from his stare and the words which he fired at her. It was only when he sighed heavily, swept his hand through his hair and turned away that she realized her legs felt like jelly and she sat, threaded her fingers together and clenched her hands, willing herself to think straight.

"Guy, we've time to sort out how we'll handle it."

He, too, had had time to think and when he turned to her, she could see the look of exasperation and disbelief had passed. "And I do need time. I'm sorry, Lucia, but this has come as a shock. I don't want an argument." He sighed. "I guess what I'm trying to say is that I want to support you, but I need you to know my stance too. I need to be assured that I will have a relationship with my child."

Her heart sank a little when she realized that his need wasn't for a relationship with her.

"A relationship with the child." She nodded. "If you still want that after the baby's born, then you'll be entitled to that."

"Entitled," he muttered under his breath. He looked away, as if he couldn't bear looking at her for a moment longer. How the hell did he expect to have any relationship when he couldn't even bring himself to look at her?

"We need to get going. Back to Wellington. I think the holiday's over, don't you?"

Sure, the holiday was over before it had even begun.

The return journey was beyond awkward. Whenever Guy glanced over at Lucia, first in the small boat to Tanakina and then in the car to the airport, she was looking away, with a cool, detached mask as if she'd closed down to the business of feeling. She'd retreated behind a wall which, Guy decided, would have made her Chinese ancestors proud. There was no breaching it, not that he wanted to. He felt as if he'd been tackled hard by a rugby forward and had been winded—physically and emotionally. It was one thing realizing he wasn't totally averse to a future with a family, it was another thing entirely to suddenly find that future beginning today.

But, as the hours passed and he drove Lucia to her apartment, a growing unease filled him. The shock of her announcement was beginning to wear off and the reality starting to sink in. The foremost of which was that Lucia was alone in Wellington, away from family, and with a new future to face. He'd said he wanted to support her, but as he went over and over in his mind what had been said, he realized he'd done the opposite—he'd acted like a total bastard.

When he stopped in front of her apartment building, Lucia gathered her bag and opened the door. He reached out to her and put his hand on her arm.

"Lucia, I—"

"Don't!" She said abruptly. "I think you've said all you had to say on the subject. There's nothing more to be said."

"I'm sorry, I—"

"You're not sorry, Guy, so don't pretend to be. You made yourself pretty clear back there. You have no interest in being a part of my life, but you insist on being a part of our child's. Well, you've a right to that. And I'll keep you informed through my lawyer."

The door slammed in his face, and he slowly dropped his head until it rested on the steering wheel. What the hell had he done?

Lucia refused to think about Guy. She refused to answer his texts or his phone calls and when he turned up at her apartment, she refused to give him admittance. As far as she was concerned, he'd said all he had to say. He only wanted her to have a relationship with the baby, and that wasn't good enough for her.

She lay awake at night, dry-eyed as she thought through what she should do. And during the day she focused on her work, and made plans for her and her child. Beginning with a doctor's appointment. Guy wouldn't be in her life. But a baby would. A baby... And then she'd fall asleep reassured by the warmth of the love of a tiny child whose love would be unconditional, and whom she could love without restraint, without fear of hurt.

A week later the doctor's examination and tests had verified her pregnancy, and it was beginning to feel real to Lucia. She had a scan booked for the following week.

She'd returned from work to be surprised by a Skype call from her mother.

"Mother!"

"Lucia, I hope you're well?"

It was the usual formal prelude to their conversations. Lucia hesitated only a moment before replying in the affirmative. She wasn't going to tell her mother about the pregnancy until the very last possible moment. She knew her mother would insist she return to Shanghai, not continue to live alone in Wellington to bring up a child.

"Good."

"And you? Is everything okay? I wasn't expecting a call today." She settled on the chair in front of the wide screen.

"It's about the painting."

"But I emailed you. It's okay; we don't need to do anything further about it."

Her mother looked grim, but then she often did. "You didn't say why."

"No, I didn't."

"Why, Lucia? I need to know."

"Because I'm no longer seeing him. I'm no longer interested in helping him with the painting."

"Ah, I wondered. Unfortunately, Lucia, it's too late to withdraw your interest."

Lucia frowned, instantly alert. "What do you mean?"

Her mother leaned forward on the mahogany desk in her office, her gaze flinty sharp. "I mean, that the businessman concerned—Mr. Zhang—has been made aware of the fact his painting isn't the original."

"How?"

"Who knows? People are always quick to pass on news to wealthy and powerful men. He's made it known that he won't let the matter rest there. I mean, Lucia, that he's aware that you've been working on the painting and knows your reputation. He believes that you'll spread the word that Guy owns the original, which will make his own worthless. He is not pleased." Her mother paused for dramatic effect. And the effect *was* dramatic inside Lucia, as a flush of adrenaline made her heart pound with a fear she hadn't experienced since she'd left Shanghai. "And I'm afraid you'll have to address this issue before..."

"Before?" Lucia had never heard her mother hesitate about anything.

Her mother licked her lips. "Before he does."

"Ah," Lucia said, sitting back. "I'll pass this onto Guy." She shrugged. "But it's not up to me."

"You need to stress to him the importance of acting on this, Lucia. You understand the seriousness of the situation?"

She did. She hadn't wanted to admit it because she didn't want to think about Shanghai and its dangers. She'd entered a new life, in a new world, and didn't want to live by the old rules, or let them interfere. She'd been living a false dream, a fool's paradise. "Yes, I do."

Her mother must have seen the change in Lucia's attitude because she relaxed, and nodded. "I'm sorry you have to do this."

"I won't be doing anything, Mother. It's Guy's painting. We're not together, so it's up to him to deal with this."

"Guy can't do this alone. He knows nothing about Shanghai, not the language, the customs, nor the people. You need to do this with him, Lucia. Mr. Zhang trusts you; he knows you're my daughter. He knows you're one of a few people who can distinguish the genuine Goldie from the fake. *You* have to do this."

Lucia shook her head, for the first time feeling tearful since Guy had left—frustrated at being forced down a path, the opposite of the one she wanted to travel. "You're telling me I have no choice."

"Not if you want to move on from this. And I want you to move on. I didn't want you to leave Shanghai, of course I didn't. But I understood your need to leave after Roberto's death. I still hope you'll return one day."

"I can't do that, Mother. I can't go back to that life."

For the first time, her mother's face showed pain. But probably only Lucia would have detected it. Her mother swallowed.

"I wish—" Her mother's words were snatched away by a gasp of breath.

Instinctively Lucia reached out toward the screen, wanting to comfort, but unable to. She withdrew her arm. "We can't change the past."

Her mother's smile was tight-lipped, controlled, but at least it was there.

"Indeed. We all have to move forward. Including you, with this matter."

Someone attracted her mother's attention, and her mother changed her demeanor instantly. "I have to go, Lucia. Talk to Guy. We—and I mean *we* because we're all implicated now—need to deal with this, not ignore it."

Lucia had no option. If her mother believed this to be serious, she had to, too. "I will."

"Good. And Lucia?"

"Yes?"

"If there's ever anything you want, anything at all, you only have to ask."

"I know."

When the screen went blank, Lucia rose and returned to the kitchen to fix herself something to eat, reflecting all the while on what her mother had said. But more than that, on what had been left unsaid. Lucia sensed danger, and she sensed her mother's fear, but she knew the fear wasn't for her mother; it was for Lucia.

After a week of trying to contact Lucia, Guy had turned up at Lucia's apartment only to be turned away at the outside entrance. He knew she was there; he'd seen her on the small deck overlooking the harbor, but she'd refused to respond when he'd pressed the phone buzzer. She'd have known who was there through the cameras, but still, she hadn't answered.

He'd got back into his car and driven off. He'd intended to return to his apartment, but it was the weekend again and instead he turned onto the motorway and kept on driving north, north to Onihau, to the estate which he'd avoided because of Hannah. For some reason he couldn't fathom, he needed to be there, to return to where he and Hannah had lived and to remember her. Because didn't all this stem from her? His love for her, not enough, and his guilt, of which he had too much.

It was mid-evening by the time he reached Onihau and instead of going directly to the estate he drove out to the small church in the country, behind which there was a cemetery.

He got out the car, feeling incongruous in his work trousers and shirt, tie pulled askew and sleeves rolled up. The grass was long and the hills, which he'd always loved, rose up golden, close by. He walked around the small white weatherboard church, one of the oldest in the district built by Scandinavian immigrants who'd traveled to the other side of the world in search of peace and a new life. The white stone angels, who guarded the graves, now weathered and strewn with cobwebs, lent a beauty and mystery to the place, which Guy felt as soon as he entered it. And he knew he'd come to the right place, led there by some healing instinct.

He didn't seek her gravestone out immediately. He looked out to the rugby grounds which separated the church from the small settlement. Some kids were kicking around a ball in the distance, and he smiled to himself. That's what he would have been doing at that age—enjoying the freedom of escaping with his mates after school to play rugby, to get into trouble, to have fun. When had the fun stopped?

He looked over to the pin oak tree, its branches drooping gracefully to the ground, sheltering a well-kept gravestone beneath it. He suddenly had a vision of Hannah sitting on the wall of the cemetery watching him playing rugby and afterward, of him joining her, and them both sinking behind the wall as dusk fell around them, hidden from the world, lost in their passion.

He'd insisted she be buried here, instead of the regimented, disconnected civil cemetery of the nearest town. She was a part of this land, like he'd been, and he couldn't allow her to rest in some place she didn't belong.

He stood at the foot of the grave. There were fresh, bright flowers in the plain jam jar placed there, no doubt, by one of her many relations. Like many Maori graves, the headstone held a photo of Hannah. The one that he and her parents had agreed on was a close-up of her in the middle of a rugby game. Her dark hair was caught in a beautiful swirl around her head, and the set of her lips and chin revealed her strong and determined nature, but her large brown eyes were facing the camera, full of light and hope and energy.

He didn't know where the sob came from, it must have been lurking in his gut all the time, because it emerged in a part-wail, part-cry. He fell to his knees beside her photo and cried, like he hadn't cried since she died, not at the funeral, and not when clearing out her things.

Eventually, the sobs subsided and he slowly became aware of his surroundings, of the rustling of the leaves in the evening breeze which had sprung up, of the shouts of the children, closer by now, and the birdsong. He reached out and touched the photograph of Hannah. "I'm sorry. I'm so sorry."

He didn't know how long he knelt there, waiting for what, he didn't know. Forgiveness? And how did he expect her to convey that? She was dead. Slowly he rose and the leaves of the trees brushed his cheek. He pushed them away and looked into its heights, suddenly realizing how much it had grown in the three years since Hannah had been laid to rest. Another breeze swept from the hills and lifted a spray of fresh green leaves which landed gently against his cheek once more. He brushed it away again. Then he heard a call and he turned around. A rugby ball rolled to his feet. He frowned and picked it up.

"Hey, mister, give us the ball."

"Where are your manners?" Guy called back.

The boy rolled his eyes. "Give us the ball. P...lease."

Guy grinned. Cheeky kid. He was about to toss it to him when he found himself drop-kicking the ball out of the cemetery and way over to the other side of the park.

The boy swore in amazement and turned to Guy with saucer eyes. "You should be on the rugby team. My dad reckons they haven't a hope next season without some good kickers."

The kid didn't wait for an answer but was off chasing the ball along with his mates. Guy watched them play before turning to look at Hannah's grave.

Nothing had happened. He hadn't known what he'd

hoped to find. But all he'd found was the tree had grown higher and mightier than he'd remembered, he'd cried for the first time since she'd died, but there'd been no message from beyond the grave. He grunted. Stupid to have expected anything. After all he didn't believe in any of that stuff, did he?

He walked away from her grave around the church. What had he expected? Her to reach out and touch him, to reassure him that she'd forgiven him? But the only touch he'd felt was the gentle brush of the fresh green leaves of the pin oak tree.

He reached the gate and unlatched it. What else had he expected? Some secret message? There was no one there to give him one. The only person he'd met was a cheeky kid with no wisdom to impart.

Guy closed the gate behind him and glanced at the tree that no longer moved, now the breeze had died down. He drew in a deep breath of the still air and turned to look at the rugby field, empty now that the kids had been called home for the night.

No, he'd received no message. But what he had received for whatever reason, was a sense of peace. And a sense of hope.

A few days later Guy was in Wellington, wishing he was in Onihau. He'd stayed in Onihau longer than he usually did and found, to his surprise, that he was reluctant to leave. But he had no choice. He'd promised Dallas he'd show up at a lunch party to play his usual role of charmer to Dallas's more blunt approach. He'd wondered if Lucia would be there. He'd continued to try to contact her from Onihau but she'd ignored his messages. So he hoped she might be there. But she wasn't. Whether Dallas had invited her and she'd declined, Guy didn't know. Because for once, Dallas didn't bring up the subject of Lucia.

The afternoon was warm and balmy and the harbor was as smooth as a millpond. He stood outside, on the edge of a group, a part of it, and yet not a part. They chatted and laughed and yet Guy felt totally disengaged. He looked through the glass doors, into the interior and watched as one particularly beautiful woman turned and caught his eye. She smiled. But it failed to connect with him, and he turned away, embarrassed. He couldn't shake himself of the vision of Lucia. He had no interest in anyone but her.

He looked once more at the glamorous crowd inside the venue. They looked unreal. And he wanted real. He turned and left down the rear steps.

The up-market streets that connected the quayside with the city were busy with late lunchers and shoppers. Guy stopped beside one vibrantly colored shop window. A hanging mobile of rainbow-colored butterflies vied with jet-fighters and Disney characters for airspace. Toys—inventive and soft—filled every space in front of a backdrop of candy-striped wallpaper and violet sprigged linen.

And it suddenly hit him, full force. Lucia was carrying *his* child. A boy who'd kick a rugby ball and give him cheek, or a girl. *His* girl.

He looked around the street quickly and then strode purposefully through the door.

Lucia tapped her foot impatiently as she waited in the café for Guy to arrive. He was late and she had her scan appointment in an hour. She hadn't wanted to meet him, not after what happened in the Sounds, but she had no choice after her mother's call. She'd decided to tell him, pass on her mother's advice, and then leave it to him. He wouldn't want to proceed, she knew that much about him.

"Lucia!" Guy smiled and sat opposite.

She didn't smile. "You're late."

"I was shopping when I received your message."

"Shopping? You don't shop."

"Not usually." He raised an eyebrow. "Do you want to know what kind of shopping?"

"No. I have no interest in your shopping. I asked you to meet me so I could inform you of something."

"Inform me?" He grinned and crossed his arms on the table, coming uncomfortably close to Lucia. "That sounds business-like."

"Because it is. It's about your painting. My mother informs me that you've run out of time. Mr. Zhang insists on an exchange."

Guy sighed. "My lawyer thinks we have a case to dispute the original sale but my parents aren't keen to pursue it. Mom's worried about the stress on dad after his recent health scare. So, yes, I guess we'll have to return the original to this Mr. Zhang." Guy sat back in his chair, looking as if he hadn't a care in the world. "I'll organize it."

"When?"

Guy shrugged. "When I get round to it."

"Guy, the man who owns what everyone believes to be the original is a powerful, unscrupulous man, well known in Shanghai. He won't wait. This has to be attended to immediately."

"Lucia, listen to me. I don't want to talk about the painting. It's not important to me. But I know now what is."

"Wonderful. And how did you achieve this enlighten-ment? Walk into the desert? Dallas talk some sense into you? Huh?"

"No," he said quietly. "I went to Hannah's grave."

"Oh." Her breath rushed out, as if she'd been punched. She could have resisted him if he'd come up with any other explanation than that.

"I've been an idiot, Lucia. A total idiot. Too busy grieving over a lost past to move on into a future I don't deserve. Please." He reached over and took her hand which she meant to resist, truly meant to, but for some reason, it remained tucked in between both his hands. "Please," he repeated, and the urgency and pleading in his eyes disinte-grated any of her remaining reserve. "Forgive me."

She wetted her lips and swallowed, trying to ignore the effect his hands were having on her body. Should she forgive him? After all, what had he done, except simply disappoint her by his reaction? And wasn't that reasonable given the abrupt way she'd told him?

"I..."

"You don't know what to do, do you? After all the things I've said about children, you must be wondering where we are now. Is that it?"

She nodded.

"I don't want to lose you, Lucia, with or without the baby."

She looked away, unwilling to let him see her reaction to the words she'd imagined him saying in her weak moments. He must have mistaken her silence for doubt.

"How can I prove it?" he muttered. He thought for a moment and then pulled a package from his pocket and handed it to her.

"What's in here?"

"Open it and see."

She pulled open a soft pink teddy bear. Then a soft blue teddy bear.

He shrugged. "I didn't know which to pick."

And at that moment she decided. It was now or never. She had to risk it. Everything. There was too much at stake not to. "Maybe I can help with that. Are you free for the rest of the afternoon?"

CHAPTER EIGHT

G uy stood leaning against the wall, watching as the doctor prepared to scan Lucia's stomach.

He felt surplus to requirements, despite Lucia's invitation for him to attend the scan. They hadn't exactly reconciled, but at least he'd made progress... she was speaking to him now.

"Comfortable, Lucia?" the doctor asked as he squeezed the gel onto Lucia's stomach.

Lucia tucked an arm behind her head and turned to look at the screen. "Yes, thanks."

"Guy?" The doctor glanced at Guy. "Why don't you sit beside Lucia? You'll get a better view then."

Guy looked at Lucia but she made no indication. "No, I can see fine from here, thanks."

The screen shivered in and out of focus. Suddenly the heart beat thudded over the amplifier.

"There." The doctor pointed to an area of the screen. "There are the hands and feet."

Guy frowned. He could only see squiggly lines moving in and out of focus. "Where?"

"And here is the head." The doctor indicated a shape that looked alarmingly large.

"My God, what's wrong with it?"

Lucia glared at him. "Nothing!"

The doctor smiled. "Lucia's right. There's nothing wrong. It looks fine. I'll take some measurements." The doctor shifted the scanner to the front of Lucia's stomach and slid it around, as they both studied the screen intently, froze the screen, and took some measurements. He shifted the scanner again, and suddenly the shape of a baby filled the screen. "The head, there, looks perfectly formed as does the spine. Yes, nothing wrong with her."

"Her?" Lucia looked at Guy.

The doctor shifted the scanner slightly and continued to stare at the screen.

"You did say you wanted to know the baby's sex and yes, your baby is definitely a girl."

His beeper suddenly buzzed. "Sorry, I'm needed in reception. I won't be a minute. I'll leave you two with a photograph of your little girl."

As the door closed, the sound of the baby's thudding heart seemed to settle into the same rhythm as Guy's own heartbeat. Neither Guy nor Lucia said a word, simply focused on the screen where they were seeing their daughter for the first time. As they watched, a photograph emerged from the machine.

Guy walked over and picked it up. He gripped the headrest behind her and cleared his throat. "It's..." He pressed his lips together and shook his head as words failed him.

"A girl," she breathed, reaching for the photo. He gave it to her, their fingers brushing. Their first contact in weeks.

"I can't believe it."

"You thought it would be a boy?"

"I... didn't think anything. I hardly believed it to be real. But now..."

"You can see it is." She smiled and handed him the photograph. He took it and tried hard to keep his emotions in check. He couldn't believe that only weeks ago he hadn't wanted this—a baby, a daughter. And yet here she was, and now he couldn't imagine life without her. He blinked and looked up to see Lucia watching him closely.

"I've behaved like an ass. If I could turn back the clock, I would."

"What would you do?"

"I'd do the same to begin with... take you out to dinner, make love all night while a storm rages around us at Lake Ferry. But then? I'd have taken you to Wellington and made love to you again, without condoms, this time trying to make you pregnant because I can't imagine not wanting this"—he tapped the photo—"now. Nor you." He reached for her hand and took it and held it tight.

"But you can't turn back the clock. What's done is done."

Guy frowned. "You won't forgive me, will you?"

Lucia looked pensive. She shook her head. "I don't know yet. You rejected me once when I told you I was pregnant. What's to stop you rejecting me again?"

"I realize you're afraid. And that's my fault. I will prove it to you, Lucia, in every way I can, every day, I'll show you that you can trust me. Okay?"

Lucia hesitated, and the doctor reappeared before she could answer. The doctor continued to take measurements while they watched in silence, awed by what they were seeing.

"Hm," the doctor said. "Based on the information

you've given me about your conception, the baby is quite small."

Lucia looked suddenly worried.

"She'll obviously take after Lucia," said Guy.

"Yes," said Lucia quickly, as if grabbing at straws. "Yes, my mother is half Chinese. My mother's mother was English," she said to Guy by way of explanation, before turning once more to the doctor. "She's tiny, smaller than me. We're all of a small build."

"Well, that could well be it." But the doctor still didn't sound convinced. He turned to Lucia. "Have you been keeping well?"

"Yes, really well."

"Have you had morning sickness?"

"Hardly at all. Just a bit queasy now and then."

"Right." The doctor looked at them both. "What I want you to do is to take things easy."

"Why?" asked Guy suddenly. "Is there a problem?"

"Not that I can see. But, with Lucia's medical history, and the smallness of the baby, it would be wise to take a few precautions."

"Like?"

"No stress. Try to take a few days off work and relax at home. Catch up on your reading. That kind of thing. And given your job as an art restorer, you might want to examine the chemicals you work with and make a few changes."

"Can you arrange that?" asked Guy.

Lucia shrugged. "Yes, I don't think there will be a problem. But I don't see there's any need. I feel fine."

"I think it will be a good idea," said the doctor.

It wasn't until they both got in the car that Guy raised it again. "You *will* take some leave, won't you?"

"I'm not sure. I'll think about it. But I feel fine."

"But the doctor said—"

"Oh, he's just careful. All he said was 'I think it will be a good idea'. Hardly warning me to slow down."

"No. I guess so. But..."

"Don't worry. I won't take any unnecessary risks."

"Good. Right, where shall we go? I think we should celebrate."

Lucia smiled and turned to him, and for the first time, Guy felt that everything might be all right. "Dinner? I'm really hungry."

"Dinner it is then."

Lucia finished her dinner and looked around the old-fashioned hotel dining room. It was in Greytown, the closest town to Onihau. Most of the town's architecture was colonial. However this hotel hadn't been gentrified; its walls were covered with old-fashioned busily-patterned wallpaper, which competed with the carpet with its brown and orange swirls. And she couldn't remember the last time she'd seen prawn cocktail on the menu.

It wasn't what she'd expected, but then she realized with Guy, that she needed to expect the unexpected.

"So, what do you think of my local?" Guy said with a grin.

"I think I've finally found the real New Zealand."

"You'd be right, there. Most people don't frequent the kind of restaurants and cafés you do in Wellington. Out here, in the country, old established hotels like this one are where most people drink."

"It's more of a bar than a hotel." She glanced at the door

to the bar through which came the sounds of people enjoying themselves.

"That's what it's become over the years."

"And this is where you used to come when you lived at Onihau?"

"Yes. With my mates."

"Except, no doubt, you were in the bar, rather than this... dining room."

"You got it!"

"Well, the food *is* excellent."

"I thought you thought that after having seen the way you demolished your dinner."

"I do not demolish my food!" she replied indignantly. "And it is very rude of you to say so."

He sat back in his chair and grinned. "I'm a New Zealander. I call a spade a spade."

"And I call it an implement to extract and transport material from one site to another," she said with a laugh.

"Then we're going to need the help of a translator in the foreseeable future."

She was suddenly serious. "You *do* see that we have a future together, then."

He paused and looked at her. "I do. You know, I used to come here with Hannah, as well as my mates."

She blinked lightly at what seemed to be a sudden change from talking about their future together, to Hannah. She took a sip of her water. "You've hardly mentioned Hannah before."

"No. But I've been thinking about her a lot lately. About what happened and about its impact on me. But that was three years ago. And for the first time, I feel a change in me."

"How?"

He sighed. "When I'm on the road to Onihau, I don't get a feeling of dread. I *want* to go there now."

"What do you feel instead of dread?"

"I feel"—he shrugged—"peaceful."

She smiled. "Peaceful is good."

"It certainly is. I chose my job because it kept me out of the country most of the time, and busy. Too busy to think or feel. But meeting you, it's well...hard to explain."

She could see the struggle it was taking for him to express his feelings, which wasn't unusual in her limited experience of men. She reached out for his hand, the first time that she'd reached out to him. He looked up with surprise and gripped her hand in his. She was still wary, still anxious to keep her heart safe. But she also recognized she had a chance here. And opening his heart to her was the one thing he could have done to unlock her own feelings.

"Try to explain. I want to hear. I want to understand."

"Meeting you, Lucia"—he rubbed his thumb over her hand with a strength which revealed the depths of his feelings—"had made me feel for the first time that life continues, that there's hope."

It might not have been a declaration of love, but Lucia wouldn't have trusted it if it had been. What Guy had said was more solid than that. It was something she, too, could believe in, and move forward with. "Me, too. For the first time since I can remember, I feel there's hope; I feel there's a future to look forward to."

Guy's features relaxed. "It seems to me that we can *do* something with hope. Move forward from there, as a family. What do you think?"

She smiled. "Yes. I think we should try." She slipped the

scan photo from her pocket and looked at it. "If not for us, then for our daughter."

Guy glanced at the photo. "She has your eyes."

Lucia laughed. "Yeah, right. One thing we can say is that she'll have my build." She paused, as she recalled the doctor's concern over her baby's size. He was simply being cautious, like all doctors. She refused to believe anything could go wrong after this near miracle of conception. The other doctors had been wrong, and this doctor could be wrong, too. A happy future was suddenly tantalizingly close. "Can we make it, Guy?"

"I don't know. But we've just seen why it's worth a try." He took the photo from her and her stomach warmed at the expression that came into his eyes. Whatever he felt for her, and she had no idea, she could see that his heart was already taken with the image in the photograph. "Just as well it's a girl. All the stuff I bought should be fine.'

"Stuff? What stuff?"

He grinned. "You'll see."

She groaned. "Not pink by any chance? Pink, frilly stuff?"

"Maybe." He looked away, a little disconcerted.

"Good. I happen to like pink, frilly stuff."

He grinned. "Excellent, then you'll like the dress I bought for you, too." His grin turned to laughter as he evidently read her change in expression accurately. "Come on, let's go to Onihau. My parents are away and I think we should have a quiet night in."

"My thoughts exactly."

"You've got to keep your energy up."

She slipped off her shoe, and smoothed her foot up his leg and enjoyed watching his eyes narrow with desire. "*Not* my thoughts exactly."

How different she felt, driving the road to Onihau now, compared to the one and only previous time she'd been there. Then, she'd only just met Guy and had been determined to keep her distance. Now? She was determined *not* to keep her distance.

The slam of the car doors closing split the empty quiet of the estate, and a waft of beautiful fragrance drifted over to Lucia. She turned to see where it was coming from. Above a gate, built in a red-bricked wall, tumbled old-fashioned roses. As Guy dealt with alarms, she wandered over to the gate and leaned on it and inhaled the delicious fragrance. In the twilight the colors had lost their color and had become luminescent under the light of the bright full moon. Tears pricked her eyes. Never had she been anywhere more beautiful—not Shanghai with its stunning towers and tropical gardens, not Italy, with its ancient buildings full of memories and stories and smell of lemons, and not England, with its history and lush green countryside. Here, there was a different quality... something fresh and new and pristine. It seemed fitting. A new start.

Suddenly she felt Guy's presence beside her. "Would you like to walk through the garden before we go inside?"

"Very much."

He took her hand and opened the gate, and they walked into a different world.

The gardens had at one time been formally planted but the roses and other scented climbers had run riot within the small garden, making the trellises invisible and the yew trees over-run with climbers.

"Mother prefers the more natural look," said Guy, by way of explanation.

They continued walking through the formal garden and out a rear gate into an olive grove. They walked under the spreading shadows of old olive trees to where the vines began. The moonlight cut a swathe of gold on the sun-dried pasture and dusted the vines with a sprinkling of the same gold.

"I thought moonlight was meant to be silver," said Lucia.

"Whoever said that hadn't seen it in mid-summer in New Zealand."

He checked the grapes. "Won't be long until harvest. They harvest in Sicily in the moonlight, you know."

"Why?"

"It's so hot there that if they picked them during the day, there's a danger they'd start fermenting before they'd even reached the cellar. Lucky for us it rarely goes over ninety degrees here."

She watched him looking around. He belonged here. She could see it in the proprietorial way he rested his hand on the pole that marked the end of a row of vines, and in his expression, as he looked across his land—it was one of profound satisfaction. He turned to look at her.

"What is it?"

"Just thinking that you look like you belong here. You look like you've grown from this soil." And she wished she had a fragment of that same solidity. She wanted it now, more than ever.

He shrugged. "I guess I do. And I guess I'm only now realizing that. I've left it too long in the hands of Dad and his managers. I'll take over the winery and the estate. I can manage the properties from here, too. Dad will be relieved."

"Your mother, too, I should imagine."

"Yes, but it's not just Onihau I want now. I want this to work for you and me. I want this to work, truly, Lucia."

"I do, too."

"Then how the hell did we get off to such a rocky start?"

"I don't know. But we have another one. Together. Hold me, Guy."

He pulled her to him and wrapped his arms around her, and she rested her cheek against his chest and listened to the beating of his heart. "I have you, now." He kissed her hair. "I have you, and I won't let go."

She lifted her head to his, and he kissed her. His lips were gentle and sensitive against hers, caressing more than demanding. But with each sweet brush of his lips against hers, each sweep of his hand over her back, she wanted more. She deepened the kiss and was rewarded with a sharp intake of breath from Guy. She moved closer to him. She wanted to feel every inch of him against her, in her.

She pulled away. "Take me to bed."

He didn't say anything, merely took her hand, and they walked quickly back, along the moon-drenched paths, following the lines of vines, half-running under the shadowy olive groves until they reached the house. They didn't stop until they reached his bedroom. Then he turned, kissed her and she surrendered to the sweetness of his kiss, the caress of his hands and an overwhelming feeling of completeness.

Lucia woke to see the sun streaming in the bedroom. She rolled over and saw Guy standing on the deck outside, fully clothed, with his back to her.

She rose from the bed and pulled on a robe, tying it as

she walked out the open doors toward him. She slipped her arms around him and rested her head on his shoulder. "Trouble sleeping?"

He smiled and dropped a kiss on her head. "Absolutely. And you know why. Still, I managed to get some shut-eye when my lover wasn't demanding my attention."

She grinned and kissed his neck. "It's your fault, I can't get enough of you."

He turned in her arms, and his eyes were distinctly dangerous. "You want to go to bed?"

"Uh-uh." She shook her head and stepped backward away from him. "I'm expecting a call from my mother. She's pressing me about going to Shanghai."

Guy frowned. "Have you told her you're pregnant?"

"No way. She'd want me to return to Shanghai permanently. She wouldn't want me here alone, bringing up a child."

"But you won't be alone."

"I hope not."

"I promise. We can move here to Onihau. Do you think you could give up your work to move here permanently? I don't want our children in apartments without open spaces to play in."

She looked around at the sunlight playing on the pool, the sage green of the olive trees and the distant gold hills.

"Guy, I've always imagined a home like this, filled with children. But I never dared to hope. What about you? No more shadows of the past?"

"They'll always be here, but I'm not running from them anymore. I think, I hope, I've finally made my peace with them."

Lucia's phone rang from inside the house. Lucia glanced toward it, her smile faltering. "Now all we have to do is tell my mother of our plans. But not yet. We'd better go back to the house. Mother texted to say she wants to talk with us both."

"That sounds ominous."

Lucia didn't answer because she thought the same thing.

"I'll run on ahead and get the call," said Guy.

"Stall her; I need to get changed."

Lucia went straight into the bedroom and could hear Guy making small talk with her mother, which she was sure her mother wouldn't appreciate. But if it bought her a few minutes to comb her hair and get dressed, it'd be worth it.

Within a few minutes, she'd followed Guy's voice into the small TV room where he'd connected her phone to the screen.

"Mother," greeted Lucia, as she sat and Guy moved away.

"Lucia. I've been having a nice chat with Guy." Lucia decoded this as her mother questioning what on earth she was doing with Guy after she'd told her that it was over.

"Yes, we're at his estate in Onihau. About an hour out of Wellington."

"That's convenient. Please, ask Guy to join us. I'd like to talk with you both."

After Guy sat, Lucia saw her mother's eyes move from one to the other, no doubt noticing how close he sat, how his leg brushed hers. Nothing escaped her mother.

"Mrs. Rossi, what's on your mind?" asked Guy.

"Please call me Mai."

Lucia raised an eyebrow. Her mother must like Guy. She didn't know anyone who called her mother, Mai.

"Mai." He smiled that completely disarming smile and she saw a glimmer of response from her mother.

"It's about your painting, Guy. The Goldie. As you're already aware, I've tracked down the owner. He's heard about Lucia's inquiries and now knows that you have the original." She paused and looked him steadily in the eye. "He wants it."

Guy shrugged. "And I guess we don't have much choice but to return it. My parents don't want to contest the original sale. They don't want the cost or stress of it all."

"Good. Because Mr. Zhang is very sure he wants this painting and I fear litigation would prove both costly and fruitless. His influence is wide. He wants you and Lucia to bring the painting here, to Shanghai. And he's *not* prepared to proceed in any other way."

Lucia felt a chill of fear run along her spine.

"I'll send someone to Shanghai with the painting, but there's no *way* we're going there," said Guy.

"Any particular reason?"

Guy looked at Lucia and then turned slowly to face her mother. "Only that we're not at Mr. Zhang's beck and call."

"Haven't I made myself clear? There could be repercussions."

"What kind?"

"Ask Lucia." Her mother's face was icy now, as was her voice. "I must go. Contact me when you've thought it through."

Her mother's image disappeared from the screen.

"Guy, maybe we should do as Mother says. She's not a scaremonger. Her world is different to the one you know."

"You have to be kidding me! Aside from the painting itself, you heard what the doctor said. You mustn't have any stress. Which means you mustn't travel, especially to Shanghai. Especially to your family, from what you've told me about your brother. For all we know this Mr. Zhang could be involved in the Triads. We could be walking into a dangerous situation."

Lucia bit her lip, thinking hard. "It'll have its risks, but honestly? Mother will make sure we're protected." She looked up and caught his eye. "As I said before, while my mother isn't part of any gang, her father—my grandfather—was. And his legacy continues on through her, whether she likes it or not. No one would dare to hurt my mother, or me, after what happened when Roberto was killed."

Guy sat back heavily. "What the hell happened?

"Okay, backing up. I had some... trouble—"

"Trouble? Now isn't the time to keep anything from me, Lucia."

She nodded; he was right. "There were a couple of men pursuing me. At first, I was vaguely flattered. But they were working together, and twice they set me up, trying to get me alone. It was clear what they wanted... what they intended. But both times they were thwarted—purely by accident. I was scared and made the mistake of telling my brother. I didn't realize these two men were in a rival triad. I didn't even know the extent of my brother's involvement. Anyway, my brother took action; he was killed. Seems my brother and his men were outnumbered. They didn't stand a chance."

Guy thrust his fingers through his hair and swore. "Lucia. This is crazy stuff!"

"Don't I know it! That's why I left. I couldn't handle it. *Any* of it."

"So why do you think things are safer now?"

"Because things changed after Roberto's death. I've been kept informed by my mother's right-hand man, Lee Kun. My mother was shattered by my brother's death and blamed herself. She called in her contacts, her network, and there was a massive shakedown within the gangs. Those two men? They're no longer around."

"No longer around?" Guy shook his head in disbelief, but Lucia could see he understood.

"Although my mother is, formally, outside the organization, no one would dare cross her now. She has too many powerful alliances inside."

Guy studied her for a moment before leaping up and pacing across the room, hands thrust in pockets. "So, you're saying it's fine for us to go because everyone's scared of your mother. You know? I find that less reassuring and more reason to stay away."

She shook her head. "It's too late for that. I'm sorry, I should never have started this whole thing. If I knew who owned the other painting, I'd have stayed away, believe me."

"But you didn't, and we can't stay away."

"That's about the sum of it."

"And what about you? What about the baby?"

She pressed her hand against her stomach. "Mother says you can't do this on your own."

"Then why can't *she* come with me?"

"She doesn't get involved at that level."

"Right. She just gives the orders. Doesn't get her hands dirty."

Lucia nodded. "If we stay here and do nothing, this *won't* go away."

"You don't know that for sure. It's a huge risk, not only walking into a world of gangs, but also for you and the baby. And it's not a risk I'm willing to take."

Lucia could see by the set of Guy's face, and his firm tone that she wasn't going to dissuade him. She'd said all she could say. But perhaps he had a point. Maybe, just maybe, things would work themselves out. After all, they *were* thousands of miles from Shanghai. And maybe Guy had a better handle on the situation that she did. She clung to that hope even while she felt a sinking in the pit of her stomach that refused to leave. And she couldn't help wondering whether *not* going to Shanghai would cause her more stress than going.

CHAPTER NINE

It could have been the fact she'd spent so much time alone growing up, creating her own world out of nothing more than her dreams, or maybe it was simply in her nature, but whatever the reason, Lucia pushed the threat to the back of her mind with relative ease.

The sun was shining, and Onihau was like some enchanting escape from the world. She could hardly imagine Shanghai and Onihau co-existing in the same world and she certainly didn't try hard to.

Guy, too, hadn't mentioned the painting, Shanghai or her mother since their conversation. And they hadn't returned to Wellington, as Lucia had expected. Guy's parents were away and it seemed Guy no longer felt it necessary to avoid Onihau. Things really *had* changed.

"If we stay here for the weekend," Guy said stretching out on the settee by the pool and putting an arm around Lucia, "we can achieve a number of things."

"Like a tan?" Lucia said wryly noting how they were both definitely *not* in "achieve" mode.

"There is that," Guy acknowledged. "And we mustn't underestimate that. Relaxing will be good for you."

"I'm fine!"

Guy lowered his sunglasses and looked at her. "More than fine."

And Lucia felt a buzz of attraction low in her stomach as his eyes raked over her body. She nudged his leg with her foot. "Focus, Guy. Tell me what we need to achieve."

He pushed the sunglasses back into place. "It involves all the things you're good at—your artistic eye, your pragmatism, and, not least, your ability to plan for the future."

"Um, intriguing. And won't you be helping me with this mystery task?"

"Oh yes. I'll be using all the things I'm good at."

"And what's that?"

"My credit card."

"What *is* this all about?"

He rose from the settee and held out his hand to help her up. "Come with me, and I'll show you."

He walked her through the house, past their bedroom to a small separate wing comprising two rooms connected by a bathroom. He opened one room and it was full of boy's toys. Airplanes hanging by invisible threads, fighting imaginary air battles; an ancient looking teddy bear, books on planes, sports trophies, posters.

Lucia leaned against the door jamb and smiled. "Your old room, I take it."

"Yes. I moved to a larger room when I was a teenager, but my mother's never had it redecorated. She forgot about it, I guess."

"I doubt it. She probably couldn't bring herself to do anything to it. It's like a time capsule. And one she wouldn't want to forget." She stepped inside and looked around, picking up a photo of Guy aged around ten, with a big gap-toothed grin, his arm casually slung around a girl. Lucia suddenly froze. She held the photo up to Guy who was watching her warily. "Hannah?"

"Yes."

"She's cute."

He nodded and took the photo from Lucia and looked at it. "She'd just thrashed me at tennis. She was always good at sports."

"And who are all these people?" Lucia pointed to a photo of a crowd of people laughing outside a Maori meeting house, its red-stained carvings framing the group.

"Hannah's family."

"What, all of them?"

"She belongs to a big local Maori family."

"Do you ever see them?"

"Oh, yes. They still invite me to their family get-togethers. I haven't been for a while, though." He set the photo down on the table and cleared his throat. "Anyway, I thought it's about time to clear this room out and make a new start. You should start planning on how to redecorate it for our daughter."

Lucia was shocked. She looked around the room, at all of Guy's history, and couldn't imagine clearing any of it away. "No! We can't do *that*."

"Why not?"

"Because...we can't turn our back on your past. We need to, I don't know, keep it with us. Incorporate it. There must be another room."

"There's the bedroom opposite. It's smaller, though."

They walked across the hall to another room, and he opened the door. Lucia stepped into the light-filled space: cream walls, soft cream carpet, built-in cupboards and large, sun-filled windows. "This is the one." She walked to the window and pushed it open. It looked out onto a lawn and garden where there was a swing and a trampoline, beyond which the vines grew. She turned to Guy. "This is perfect. We'll use this as her bedroom. And, who knows, in the future, we may use your old room for a son."

She was rewarded with a beaming smile from the heart and she knew by that alone, that Guy was ready for this. "You can't go wrong with paint," said Guy casting his eye around the walls. "Just needs freshening up."

"No way! We're expecting a girl and she'll need it to be lovely. I'm thinking flowers, something really pretty. What do you think?"

"I think you can have whatever you like. I'll call the decorators in on Monday."

"No, I want to do it."

"I'm not having you climbing ladders."

"Guy. I'm going to do this."

"No way. What you can do is select the stuff. What you can do is shop for everything and then I'll do the rest. Okay?"

She shrugged. "Okay." He was right; she wasn't going to take any risks. But shopping she could do. Shopping, she could *definitely* do.

Greytown was busy with the usual weekenders having brunch and browsing the antique, gift and dress stores in the beautifully restored nineteenth-century buildings which lined its central street. The historic town was the closest to Onihau and the perfect place for Lucia to find bits and pieces to fill the nursery.

They emerged from one shop and bumped into a man of around Guy's age, who greeted Guy with a big bear hug, and an elderly woman, who was bent nearly double.

"Hey, Guy!" his friend laughed. "About time we caught up, mate! But you're never around."

"I'm here this weekend."

"And is this your new lady?"

"Yes, this is Lucia. Lucia, this is Tane."

"Ah, Lucia," he half-sang in an opera-like way. "Good to meet you, girl. Hope we'll get to see you more often than we've seen Guy lately."

"You will," replied Guy. "We're planning on moving to Onihau full time as soon as we can settle things in Wellington.

"Woo-hoo, great news." He turned to the old lady on his arm. "Aunty!" he said loudly. "It's Guy and his lady. They're moving into Onihau together."

"Guy?" The old lady lifted her face and Lucia could see that she was partly blind, her eyes filmy. She was reminded sharply of another painting by Goldie. The woman even had a moko—a tattoo around her chin and mouth. She was stunning. "How are you, boy?" Aunty might be physically frail, but her voice emerged loud and clear.

"All the better for seeing you, Aunty," Guy said kissing both her cheeks. Aunty took hold of his hands with a firm grip.

"And you have a lady?" She peered around, her eyes narrowing as she tried to decipher her surroundings.

"I do indeed. Lucia."

"Come here, girl, and let me see you."

Lucia took the old lady's reaching hand in hers and tried not to wince under her too-firm grip. "You be good to this boy, you hear? He's a fine lad. And he made a loving husband to my mokopuna."

"That's grandchild," explained Guy.

"Ah, you are Hannah's grandmother. Pleased to meet you Mrs—"

"Call me Aunty. Everyone does."

"Because she looks after everyone," her grandson added.

"If they could look after themselves, then I wouldn't have to do it for them," said the old lady sharply. She tugged on Lucia's hand which was still very firmly in the old lady's grip. "You must come and visit me, child. Let me get to know you. And you can get to know us. We're still Guy's family—and yours now—even if Hannah is no longer with us." She squeezed Lucia's hand in emphasis and focused closely on Lucia's eyes. "Don't forget. Come and visit me."

Lucia was touched by the woman's request. "Yes, I will, thank you."

Aunty then released her grip on Lucia, and the conversation turned to Guy.

After they had said their goodbyes, they walked across the road and into a café. They took a seat in the garden, separated from the footpath by neatly boxed hedging. A spreading plane tree gave them protection from the sun.

He gave an order to the waiter and sat back and looked at her. "So, what did you think of Aunty?"

"She was... amazing. If not a little daunting."

He laughed. "I know. She's blazed a trail through her life, and everyone else's, all right. She's a straight-talker and worked for the Ministry of Education for many years, making sure that the Government did right by Maori kids."

"Wow! I hadn't imagined that."

"She doesn't look like a typical civil servant, and she never tried to. She was always true to herself."

"That's not so easy to be."

"She took a shine to you. You should go and visit her some time."

"I'm not sure. I don't feel I belong, or fit into her world. Maybe she was simply curious about me."

"You heard what she said. I married her granddaughter. Therefore I'll always be a part of her wider extended family, as will anyone connected with me. That's the way it is."

"Maybe for her. But I find it hard to think, or feel, like that."

"Give it time."

She nodded, scared that now she'd found the place she wanted to be, that either it was too late for her to put down roots, or something else, something that the twist in her gut reminded her of, would prevent her. She smiled at Guy, determined to ignore the fear.

Lucia should have known that he wouldn't let her climb a ladder. Instead, she spent most of Sunday relaxing by or in the pool, as Guy cleaned the paintwork and prepared the walls for the wallpaper.

She heard a curse word coming from inside the house and smiled to herself. It wasn't the first, but Lucia knew better now than to ask if he needed help. Instead, she went for a swim. The sun was hot on her skin, but the water was refreshing and a sparkling blue. The cicadas throbbed in the trees, and the air shimmered over the rows of grapevines leading off toward the narrow strip of blue sea. It was a perfect place to raise children. But she still felt that niggle inside that refused to leave. She closed her eyes tight against the bright light. It was so close, this land of safety and security, this place which held everything she'd always wanted. Her hand grasped the water, and when she lifted it out, the water drained away, leaving her palm empty.

Suddenly Guy appeared and dived into the water, rocking her on the water's surface.

He swam to her and kissed her cheek. "It's done!" He kissed her stomach. "Baby, if you only knew what I've gone through to bring pink flowers into your life."

Lucia laughed, her fears forgotten. "She might not, but I do."

Much later, they lay side by side on the wide couch, watching night slowly fall on the hills around them, talking, caressing, each of them slowly believing that what was happening was real.

Before they went to bed, they wandered into the nursery which was all prepared, ready for decorating.

"I can't imagine this. I can't imagine a baby here. It feels like a dream."

Lucia shivered. "Don't say that."

Guy put his arm around her. "It's just happened so fast, and I have no imagination whatsoever."

"I can help you. Stay there."

She quickly retrieved some of her shopping bags and returned to the nursery. "I'll show you some of the things I bought." She reached into the bag and brought up some parcels wrapped in tissue.

"Let me guess. Pink hearts? The essential ingredient for a girl's bedroom. Or a Disney-singing mobile?"

"Wrong on both counts."

She slowly unraveled the mobiles and unusual decorations she'd discovered, and laid them on an empty shelf, describing how they could be used. Guy opened the French doors and they sat on the step, talking.

"What's that other parcel in your bag?"

She carefully unwrapped it and placed the contents on the step beside them.

He picked one up. "Lead soldiers? I haven't seen one of these in years. You're taking this non-sexist toy thing to heart, aren't you?"

She laughed. "I bought these for *me*. They remind me of when I was little. My brother used to play with them." She held one up to the light and twisted it so she could see every color of the uniform, every finely molded line. "Roberto had whole regiments of them. He used to line them up in different formations. He'd spend hours playing with them."

Carefully, she wrapped up the pieces again. Guy reached across and placed his hand on hers. "What was Roberto like?"

She flashed him a quick, uncertain smile. "He was younger than me by two years." She paused while she finished putting away the soldiers.

"Go on."

She sucked in a raw breath. "He looked like my father—tall and strong, but that's where the resemblance ended. He was studious, quiet and... troubled. In Shanghai, my mother tried to keep their lives separate from her family's... business. She thought she'd succeeded. She didn't realize he'd joined them. She'd kept her distance so well that no one told her." Lucia grimaced. "She no longer keeps her distance."

"You said she's an art dealer?"

"Yes. But she's connected with the family business

again. Not in a big way, but enough to protect her family." She turned to Guy. "Enough to make sure nothing will happen to us in Shanghai."

"We won't be testing that because we're not going to Shanghai. Nothing will make me change my mind."

"That's fine with me." And it was. She didn't want to return to Shanghai. She'd found an authentic life for herself here, in New Zealand, not the soap opera life she'd led in Shanghai. She hated the thought of returning. But even while she agreed with Guy, even as he pulled her to standing and kissed her, she felt an unease which refused to leave. She had a horrible feeling that Guy was wrong— something *might* happen to change his mind.

They'd stayed another day at Onihau, reluctant to leave, and the sun was setting by the time they reached Lucia's apartment building.

Guy parked immediately outside the entrance. People were everywhere on the waterfront, enjoying the still evening, and the tail end of the weekend. A few rollerbladers sped by, and the sound of laughter reached them from one of the waterside bars.

"Are you sure you don't want me to come in with you?"

Lucia looked at her windows which reflected the orange sky. They looked blank somehow. After the weekend of enjoying Guy's company, of imagining a future—for the three of them—at Onihau, she felt a weird kind of dread at the thought of returning to an empty apartment.

"I'll be fine."

"I *know* you'll be fine. But I'd like you to be more than

fine, and I'm happy to stay with you. I can go to my apartment later to grab a few things for the week."

"No really. I—"

She forgot whatever she was going to say as his fingers brushed back her hair and caressed her cheek. "Lucia... don't go all polite on me. I want you to tell me what you truly want. I want you to make demands on me. Yes?" She sighed and leaned in to him, as his fingertips sent shivers racing through her body, making her think of a lot of advantages to him coming upstairs with her now.

She took the palm of his hand and kissed it, and when she raised her eyes to his, she saw an answering lust. He slipped his hand behind her neck and gently pulled her to him and kissed her. They knew each other now, recognized the signals, and this was no tentative kiss, but a deep and sensual promise of what was to come.

When eventually they pulled apart, both were panting with desire.

"Upstairs." She kissed him again. "Now."

"Um..." He slipped his tongue between her lips and she parted her mouth for him, completely seduced by the slick movement of his tongue against hers. "*That* is more like it. I can't resist a bossy woman."

He parked the car and they went into the imposing foyer, half-running, hand in hand. They slowed to a sedate walk as the elevator opened and an elderly lady and a dog walked out.

"Good evening," the lady said.

"Good evening, Mrs. Wheeler." Lucia tried to keep a straight face and managed it until they'd got into the empty elevator and the doors slid closed. As soon as that happened their laughter was extinguished by their kisses. He balled up her hair in his hands as they pulled apart. "Lucia, I want you so badly."

The elevator dinged, and the doors opened onto the hall of Lucia's apartment. They stumbled into the foyer, mouths hot against each other. It was only when she pulled away that she opened her eyes. And what she saw in the living room made her cry out.

"What's up?" muttered Guy, busy trailing kisses down her throat.

"Stop! Guy, look!"

He pulled away from her and twisted around, following her gaze out across her living room. Instead of the usual immaculate arrangement of furnishings, her things were strewn everywhere. Clothes, taken from cupboards and drawers, were thrown randomly, some torn apart; ornaments and china smashed; paintings on the wall slashed.

She leaned against the wall, suddenly weak. This couldn't be happening. She pressed her face against his chest for a few moments and then looked again. It was still there—a scene of utter chaos and destruction. She cried out again and pulled away from Guy, but he held her back.

"No, stay. There might be someone here still."

He picked up a heavy lamp.

"No, Guy. I'll call the police." She fumbled in her handbag for her phone. "Let's get out and wait for them to arrive," she said in a hushed tone.

He pressed the elevator button, and the doors slid open and he gestured for her to go, but she shook her head. There was no way she was going to leave him alone.

He shook his head with frustration but left her where she was and walked into the living room. She pulled out her phone and dialed emergency services. As she told the police what had happened she watched Guy first walk into one room, then another, making sure all was clear.

He returned and replaced the lamp on the table.

"No one here." He pulled her into his arms, and she fell against him, shaking.

"Thank God you weren't here when it happened."

She swayed, suddenly feeling weak and sick.

He pulled away and looked at her. "You're pale. Let's get you out of here."

"No. I just need a glass of water. I want to see what they've done, what they were after."

She wandered into the living room as Guy fetched her a glass of water. She held her head, willing the panic and nausea to subside. "This all looks senseless. I can't see anything's gone. I didn't have that much stuff to begin with."

He brought it over to her, and she took a sip. He shook his head. "What a mess. Did you have anything of value here? Does it look like anything's missing?"

She wiped her eyes. "Not in here. Destroyed, yes, but not taken." She took another drink and then rose.

"Don't touch anything. The police will need to check for prints."

She walked around, checking. Then it hit her. She looked up at him suddenly. "Guy!"

"Did anyone know you'd be out? How the hell did they get through your security?"

"Guy," she repeated. "I think I know. There's only one answer."

"You know who did this?"

"I think so."

"Who?" He picked up his phone. "Tell me, and we'll get

the police onto it right away. The sooner they act, the sooner we'll catch them."

She placed her hand over the phone. "No. We can't tell the police my suspicions. Because there's nothing that can be done. Not by them."

"Why not?"

"I think they must have been after the painting. I think they must have been watching me."

"They?"

"The Chinese businessman who owns the forgery. I think his people must have decided to come here and take what they believe to be theirs. Maybe they thought the print was the original, until they could see it close up. The print-maker's sticker is a giveaway."

Guy swiped his hand over his eyes and shook his head. "This isn't going to go away, is it?"

Lucia shook her head. She felt sick inside with an invasive nausea that she could only put down to the massive sense of violation by people from a world she'd thought she'd successfully left long ago. A world, it seemed, from which she could run, but not hide.

CHAPTER TEN

After the police had left, Lucia sat on the settee and surveyed the damage. She felt numb.

"What a mess!" Guy said as he lifted the heavy cabinet which had been emptied and then thrown onto the floor.

"At least they didn't get your painting. And there's no way they can access the vaults at the gallery."

"I don't give a damn about the painting. They can have it for all I care."

"But it's valuable."

"And so is your life, believe it or not."

She looked down and twisted her hands. What had she done? She'd thought she'd left all of this behind her. And if she hadn't allowed her obsession with paintings to overtake her common sense, she would have done. But she didn't, and she had to accept the consequences. "I'm sorry."

Guy swung round to face her. "Why are you sorry? You've nothing to be sorry for."

"For getting you into this mess. You're right. I should have left the painting alone. I should have thought it through. But I just get this compulsion with artwork. Call it professional pride, or just plain stubbornness. But I can't bear to think of someone owning an original and it not being acknowledged as such."

He put his hand on her shoulder, and she placed her hand on his. "Don't worry about it. It's done. And we have to move on from here. Beginning with your apartment." He moved away, leaving her feeling strangely bereft. "I'll arrange for some people to come and tidy this for you."

"I'll do it."

"No, you won't. And before you say anything, you're not staying here, either. They've been here once, they could come again. It doesn't seem your security system is up to par."

"I'll get it updated. I should have done it when I moved in. I didn't imagine anything like this could happen in New Zealand."

Guy grunted, as he paced the untidy floor. "It happens. We'll spend the night in my apartment on the other side of town."

"They don't want *me*, don't you understand? They want the painting. I'll be fine here now that they know the painting isn't here."

"What if they decided to change tactics? What if they thought, 'We can't get the painting, we'll get Lucia instead?'"

"And do what?"

"How the hell should I know? Blackmail your mother, blackmail me? Demand the painting, demand a million dollars for your safe return? I don't know! But if they're up for doing something like this, then they'll be up for anything!"

Lucia was silent. Guy was right. They'd stop at nothing. There was only one answer. She rose and reached for her phone. "I'm ringing my mother. This has to stop now. And there's only one way to do it."

He shook his head. "We're not going to Shanghai. It's out of the question."

"There's no other way, Guy. I should have listened to my mother before. She knew something like this could happen."

"I don't want you going, Lucia. Remember what the doctor said? No stress."

"I think it's already too late for that. I need to call Mother."

"You'll tell me what she says?"

"Of course." She walked out onto the balcony as she dialed her mother's number and then turned to Guy. "They won't stop until they get it. And until they do we'll both be living each day wondering whether today's the day when we come back to something like this."

"Do you truly believe this won't stop until we do?"

"I *know* it won't." She twisted around. "Mother? Yes, hello, I know. Yes, something has happened. Something I need to talk to you about."

Guy watched Lucia close the balcony door behind her as she talked with her mother. He couldn't hear what she was saying. For some reason, she didn't want him to listen to their conversation, but he could hear the tone of her voice—tense, low and urgent—and that told him all he needed to know.

She had a past and a family, and a life in Shanghai of which he had the barest knowledge. And, for some reason, she wanted it kept that way. And he *should* respect that, except every instinct inside him screamed at him to destroy every barrier between them so he could protect her completely. She was his woman now, and he'd do anything to make sure she, and their baby, were protected.

She finished the call and came inside. "It's sorted. Mother's organizing a plane for us."

"Good."

"And it'll be a short stay. She'll make sure it goes smoothly."

"There's no other way?"

"No. I'm sorry."

He nodded. "Okay, let's get out of here."

Guy turned off the busy road in a colorful suburb and drove his Porsche into a run-down corrugated iron garage behind a row of shops which must have been part of the original settlement of Wellington.

Lucia had expected an expensively cool bachelor pad. She smiled to herself for the first time since the robbery. She turned to him with a raised eyebrow, unable to hide her surprise. "*This* is your place?"

"Yes, I inherited it from an aunt and lived here while I was at university. And then later... after Hannah died, I came back. It's full of memories. Mostly good."

They left the garage, and he padlocked it and looked at the tall old building, extending over three floors.

"It's an ex-warehouse and factory. The factory was downstairs, stockrooms up." He unlocked the door, flicked on the lights, and stood aside. "After you."

She stepped into another world. The vast space was like a massive den, complete with untidy piles of books, hi-tech gadgets and comfortable leather chairs. "It's certainly different." She picked up a crocheted cushion. "Don't tell me you made this? Or even bought it?"

"My *grandmére*. She reckoned the place needed a woman's touch and she made enough of them."

"So I see." The cushions were incongruously strewn across the masculine leather settees which were set on dark-painted boards, bearing scars of the factory setting. Built-in furniture vied for space with other, junk shop finds. A large TV was fixed at one end of the room on the bare brick wall, and black and white photographs were framed on the other walls.

"Sorry, it's a bit untidy." He grimaced as he looked around the room. "I usually only use this place as somewhere to lay my head when I'm in Wellington. I don't often entertain here anymore."

"It's fine. It's more than fine. It's perfect. It's very... you."

A slow-spreading grin supplanted his frown. "I'm perfect now, am I?"

"Just a turn of phrase. Don't let it go to your head."

"I'll try, but I can't promise anything. I've got all sorts of things going through my head at the moment."

The heat in his eyes made it pretty clear what he was thinking. It made her forget everything, including the need to be strong. She suddenly felt exhausted. "I hope it includes a chair because I'm still feeling shaky."

Guy's smile instantly turned to concern. "Of course. I'm sorry, come rest while I get us a drink."

As she put her feet up on the couch, she watched him move around the kitchen. She suddenly remembered her father doing the same thing. She imagined her father's warm, loving smile. His work had meant he was away a lot, which was why she'd had to go to boarding school. But when they'd been together—right up until he died when she was seventeen—she'd never been left in any doubt as to how much he loved her.

The connection between her father and Guy was the final blow to the wall she'd erected to keep her safe. When he brought her a hot drink and a roughly cut sandwich which would have been better used to keep a door open, she reached up and took his hand. "Thank you."

He glanced at the sandwich. "It's not much. Just Vegemite and cheese. I've limited vegetarian options, I'm afraid."

She grinned. "No, thank you for being so considerate."

He sat and put his arm around her. "Not *so* considerate, Lucia. And you know it. I've been a total fool. About the painting—I should have realized the consequences—and about you."

Suddenly there was only one thing she wanted, and it wasn't a sandwich. She put the plate down. "Guy?"

He sat opposite her and took her hands. "Yes?"

"Take me to bed."

He took her hand and led her up the long flight of stairs to the top floor. He pushed open a door to reveal uncurtained windows, the room lit by the streetlight outside.

Lucia walked into the room and looked around. It had the ubiquitous boy stuff of TV and sound system, but the main feature was the bed, large and low and totally inviting.

Suddenly there was a shout from the street below and Lucia gasped. But the shout was followed by laughter and a door banged as a group of people left a café.

He pulled her to him and held her close. "Don't worry. You're safe here. I won't let anything happen to you."

It was an impossible lie, but he didn't know it. She

wasn't safe anywhere, and that was the message she'd received loud and clear from the robbery.

"I want to believe you... but you don't know—"

He cut off her words with his finger, held against her lips. "Don't say another word. There will be plenty of time for talking later."

"But—"

He pressed his mouth to hers and his insistent lips, moving over, caressing hers, swept any further thought from her mind. By the time he'd carried her over to the bed and they'd fallen onto the soft duvet together, she'd forgotten her fears.

Lucia awoke to find the streetlight shining into the room, across her naked breasts, and her fears re-surfaced. A bus stopped close by, the dull rattling of its windows filling the quiet night. People shouted goodnight to their friends before it pulled off, dimming the streetlight briefly as it passed by.

Guy traced his finger around her breasts. "You're awake."

"Um."

He propped his head on his hand, while he continued to explore her breasts with his other hand.

"Everything okay?" he asked.

"Seriously?" she grinned. "With you doing that, *every-thing* is okay."

"I can't continue to do this, day and night, though. At some point, we'll have to talk about that mysterious phone call with your mother. About what plans you've made."

Suddenly the feeling of well-being slipped away. "Ah, that."

"Yes, that."

She suddenly felt a little queasy, and she swung her legs onto the floor.

"We can't put off this conversation forever."

"It's not that." She brushed the hair from her face and swallowed. "I don't feel so good. Must have been the scare, I guess. I need a glass of water."

"You stay there. I'll get it."

She got back into bed and sat up, her arms around her knees, listening as Guy went downstairs and moved around the kitchen. It was ridiculous how safe she felt here, with him, while she knew full well she wasn't. When he entered the room, she caught his eye and he frowned, placed the glass beside her and sat on the bed.

"Are you going to tell me your mother's plans now?"

She took a sip of water and nodded. "Just wondering where to start."

"Start with what you intend to do tomorrow."

She gave a brief smile. "Right. Tomorrow Mother's arranging flights for us to Shanghai. We'll go straight to see Mother and then on to meet Mr. Zhang, the man who thought he owned the original. Mother tried to persuade him that an intermediary would do, but he wants me because I'm the only one who knows the difference between the forgery and the original."

He rose and walked around the bed, then stood in front of the window looking across to the lights of Wellington, hands on hips and completely naked. Lucia let her eyes drift over the shadows of light and dark that played on his shoulders and back from the movement of a tree outside the window. He was strong, physically and mentally strong, but he still wasn't a match for the people they'd be dealing with in Shanghai.

She rose and came to him. "Seriously, I'll be fine."

"I don't like it. Any of it." His face was grim.

"Guy, we need to end this."

"Just send the damn painting to them if they want it so much."

"There are ways of doing business which, as a foreigner, you don't understand. But my mother does, and I trust her judgment. We have to do this. Besides my mother will make sure everything is set up properly. We'll be fine. Now"—she took hold of his hand, pushed her fingers through his and gripped his hand and tugged—"come to bed."

"Bed? Are you trying to distract me?"

She opened her eyes wide in mock innocence. "Maybe. Would that be so bad?"

"This isn't the end of it, Lucia. We'll discuss this whole thing further tomorrow. There must be another way."

"Okay." She smiled and put her arms around his neck and pressed her body against his. "So what do you want to say?"

He caressed her back and lower but, it seemed, he was not to be distracted. "If we have to go, I'm not going to leave your side. I'll be with you every step of the way, no matter what you or your mother want, or have planned."

She bit her lip and nodded reluctantly. "You can come, but you must leave me to do the business."

"No way. I'm not leaving your side until we're safely back in New Zealand, with the painting sorted. You see, I can't risk it, now. I can't risk you."

She swallowed a lump in her throat. She refused to cry. Instead, she kissed him again in wordless agreement. It seemed that Guy understood and, at last, he allowed his focus to stray to more sensuous matters.

———

Afterward, Lucia lay awake watching the dark of night slowly turn into the soft gray of morning. It wasn't restlessness which kept her awake but fear. Fear of the journey ahead.

Her cheek was on Guy's chest, and she heard the steady beat of his heart and knew that her life had become far more complicated. It wasn't because of the painting; it wasn't that she had to return to Shanghai—the place which she'd left with her mind and body barely intact—no, it was because she'd involved this man and she'd lied to him.

This trip would be dangerous. Triply dangerous now that she not only risked herself, but also Guy, and her baby.

CHAPTER ELEVEN

L ucia stared with regret at Wellington harbor and the surrounding hills as the plane roared off the runway. She felt nauseous and it had nothing to do with the pregnancy. She took a deep breath. She had to keep it in check—the fear which threatened to take hold every time she thought of Shanghai.

She had to keep cool. Real cool. Because she couldn't let the fear take hold, or else she wouldn't be able to do what she had to do. For Guy's sake. She glanced at him.

He sat opposite her in the jet's cabin, scrolling through his laptop, jabbing in the occasional response, absorbed in his business and oblivious to his surroundings.

His brows were knitted and his mouth firm in his concentration. Perfect control. Then her eyes wandered to his thick hair, pushed off his face by the occasional thrust of his fingers. Just the thought of what those fingers were capable of inspiring made her temporarily forget her fears and think of other things entirely. He looked up and caught her gaze.

"You looked flushed. You want the air conditioning turned up?" He motioned to the steward.

"No." She cleared her throat of its huskiness. "I'm fine. A woman's temperature increases when she's pregnant."

He grunted. His expression barely changed, but she could see from the look in his eyes that he knew exactly what she was thinking. "Are you sure that's all it is? Maybe you'd like a little rest in the bedroom?"

She considered his suggestion. It would certainly take her mind off what lay ahead. "It's certainly tempting."

"May as well make use of your mother's generosity," he added.

She frowned as the thought of her mother made her fears return. "I should have insisted we travel by a commercial flight."

"No, you shouldn't. The doctor said that you have to take things carefully and this is the best way for you to fly. It would take over fifteen hours to fly commercial. Even though it's nearly a dozen hours this way, it's much more comfortable."

"You didn't say anything to my mother, though, did you? I don't want her to know."

"How could I? I haven't had a chance to speak with her."

Lucia was satisfied. "Good. And you promise not to tell her about the baby?"

"Of course, if that's what you want. But she is your mother. Don't you think she has a right to know? Don't you think she'd be happy for you?"

"You don't understand my family."

"How can I, when you hardly tell me anything about them?"

She shrugged. "My family is complicated."

He leaned forward. "And we've enough time to do complicated." He sat back again. "Tell me what happened to you. Tell me how come your mother didn't take you with her to Shanghai."

She felt the instant stab of pain at the memory. But it was time. She wrung her fingers, fiddling with her rings as she thought how to begin.

He took her hand and held it lightly. "It's okay, Lucia. You're safe here. Just tell me how your mother and father ever got together in the first place."

She nodded. "It was in England. My mother and father met at Oxford University. They fell in love and married. My father said it had all seemed so simple, so easy at first. But as soon as their families became involved life became more complicated. After they moved to Italy and my father had to spend so much time away with work, things became impossible for my mother."

"Why? Weren't your father's family supportive?"

Lucia pursed her lips and shook her head. "My grandmother and my father's eldest sister didn't approve of my mother. They made life difficult for her." Lucia shrugged. "Things worsened between my mother and father and they... drifted apart."

Guy nodded. "And your mother wanted to return to China."

"Yes. Her parents were pressing for her return, and it seemed the simplest option in the end. For her anyway." She looked up at Guy. "When I found out she was leaving I told her I hated her. I told her I loved my father more."

"But you were, what, around six years of age, right?"

She gave him a brief smile.

"Kids say stuff they don't mean. Your mother wouldn't have believed that you really felt that way."

"At the time, I believed she did because she left the following day, without me, taking my little brother with her." She was silent. "I've never forgiven myself."

"You were a child," Guy repeated. "I'm sure your mother thinks there's nothing to forgive. She would have understood."

"Yes, she's said as much. But it wasn't her who I hurt the most. It was me. You'd have thought I'd have learned to keep quiet about things, but I'm obviously a slow learner. After my father died, I returned to Italy. I discovered my cousin was stealing from my Grandmother and made the mistake of telling her. The family closed ranks, grandmother was furious and refused to believe me. That's how I ended up in Shanghai."

"And that's how you ended up keeping things close, because every time you opened up your heart, you were rejected."

"It took something else before I came to believe the only way to keep safe was to keep everything to myself."

"And that was when you told your brother about those men who were bothering you. You told him, and he and his men took action, which led to his death. It was the final act of loss which drove you into yourself."

She nodded. "I guess. I'm terrified that any time I open my mouth and say what's in my heart, say what's truly in my mind, everything goes wrong."

"Not this time. Not with me. When all this is over, we're going home, to New Zealand, where we'll marry and live together happily ever after. You, me, and our children. Right?"

She brushed away an errant tear. Her perfect future... all in a few sentences... and uttered by someone else. "Right," she said from between trembling lips.

"Lucia, from the moment I first saw you I couldn't keep my eyes off you."

She laughed and swept her fingers under her eyes to erase the tell-tale signs of tears. "Yes, I remember. Every time I looked at you, you were checking out a different part of my anatomy."

"Um..." He looked at her hands and turned them in his. "I was pretty taken with your wrists if I remember." He twisted her arm round gently and brought it to his lips. "Pale and delicate – I can see your veins and your heart pumping through the skin. Is it as sensitive as it looks?" His eyes looked to hers.

She swallowed. "Shouldn't think so."

He kept his eyes fixed on hers as he grazed his lips across her wrist, inhaling as he moved.

She shivered with arousal and saw his face register amusement and something more.

He lowered her hand onto the table. "I think, Lucia, that you should follow doctor's orders and have some bed rest. Some very gentle, very prolonged bed rest."

"With you?"

"Most definitely with me."

The moment they stepped off the plane, Guy knew Lucia had been economical with the truth. Her mother had to be more involved with the family "business" than Lucia had described. All eyes were on them, but it was their expression that got to Guy—a mixture of respect, anxiety and... fear.

An immaculate looking man stepped forward and greeted Lucia. "So good to see you again, Miss Lucia."

"Thanks, Lee. This is Guy Martin. Guy, this is Lee Kun, my mother's right-hand man."

They shook hands.

"You have the painting?"

"Mother's flight manager has it."

"Good." Lee Kun motioned to one of his men who took the painting from the steward. "Please, this way."

To Guy's surprise Lee opened a door marked private.

"Where are we going?" he asked.

Lee turned to him with a polite smile. "I've been so bold as to make certain arrangements for you. It will simply mean you can go through customs privately, without the bother of queueing up with the others. I hope that meets with your approval?"

"Sure."

Lee went ahead.

"Lucia, how the hell did he manage that?"

"Ah, well, that comes down to my mother again. I told you she has influence."

"Influence?" Guy repeated wryly.

Lucia didn't reply, but her quick, wary glance told him all he needed to know. He shook his head and wondered what the hell he'd got himself into.

Once out of the airport they drove into Shanghai proper and along the western bank of the Huangpu River. Opposite were the skyscrapers of Pudong District, but it wasn't there they were going. They pulled up outside an old colonial palace in The Bund, one of Shanghai's oldest areas, and were ushered into an ornate reception room.

"Looks like a palace," said Guy as he walked through the formal space richly furnished with French gilt chairs and a gleaming mahogany table in the center.

"That's because it was."

He glanced at an elaborately formal oil painting which dominated the room. "Even has its own royal family. Who owns this place? And why are we meeting your mother here?"

Lucia walked to the painting which depicted a family group, two children, and a mother and father. It was obvious that the mother was the dominant one as far as the artist was concerned.

"That's her, there."

Guy looked more closely at the portrait. He recognized her now. The woman was a more Chinese version of Lucia. "Of course it is."

"And that's my little brother and me."

He shook his head and looked around. "And don't tell me, this is home."

Lucia reached out and traced the features of her brother. "Of course."

Guy came up behind her. "You miss him."

She turned abruptly to him. "Yes, I miss him every day. And he'd be here now, if he hadn't got sucked into this damned world my grandfather created."

"And which you benefited from." A cool, imperative voice came from behind them. They both turned to see a slender woman, nearly the same height as Lucia, looking at them. "Don't forget that, Lucia."

"Mother! I didn't hear you come in."

"Obviously." The tension suddenly broke and Lucia's mother opened her arms. "It's good to see you."

The two women embraced, and Guy was struck by how similar they looked.

"Mother, I'd like to introduce you to Guy."

"Pleased to meet you..." Guy hesitated trying to figure out how you greeted someone like this.

"Please, call me Mai."

"Mai." She extended her hand and they shook hands formally. This woman wasn't someone you took liberties with.

"Welcome, Guy. Please, come and sit." She nodded to her assistant and a door opened, and three women came in carrying trays.

There was silence while the tea was organized. Then Lucia's mother nodded to Lucia who sat forward and poured three cups of tea. She handed one to her mother first, and then to Guy, with a brief, sympathetic smile. He sat back and took a sip of his tea. He felt as if he'd walked into a play with no knowledge of the script.

Guy suddenly realized that, as far as Lucia's mother was concerned, he was merely an accessory, tolerated only because of Lucia. And that was fine with him. Except she was wrong. He did have a function and that was to make sure Lucia stayed safe.

"You are well, Lucia?"

"Yes thanks, Mother. The flight was long but comfortable."

"Thank you for the plane, it was very thoughtful and much appreciated," he said.

Her mother turned to Guy, her expression unchanging and unreadable. Guy wished he hadn't worn a jacket. Even with the air conditioning, he felt himself sweat under her laser-like stare.

"You are welcome."

When her gaze shifted from him, he sighed with relief. She might look like Lucia, but he thanked God that Lucia had only a shadow of her mother's intensity. And that shadow was more than enough for him.

"Now." Lucia's mother took a sip of her tea and then sat

against her hard-backed chair, looking every inch the powerful empress. "Perhaps you will tell me about this painting."

"Well—" began Lucia.

Her mother raised a hand. "I'd like Guy to tell me."

Of course she would. "It's been in my family for over a hundred years. My great-great-grandfather commissioned Goldie to paint his new wife, my great-great-grandmother."

"Then how is it that a wealthy businessman in Shanghai now claims to own it?"

"My father sold it. Or at least he thought he did. There must have been some mix-up."

"No doubt it was the head of your family. A change of heart."

"No. It wasn't my father. He's not like that."

Lucia's mother exchanged a knowing glance with Lucia and looked at Guy. "It doesn't matter who it was. The fact remains you have the original, and Mr. Zhang is not pleased. Apart from the fact he paid for the original, he's more appalled by the loss of face. Something you should understand, Lucia."

"I do. You have arranged a meeting?"

"Yes. Lee Kun will accompany you on my behalf."

"Hold on a moment, I'm going too," Guy said. "It's my painting, and I'll take responsibility for the exchange."

The two women exchanged looks and Lucia's mother inclined her head. "As you wish. I appreciate your care for my daughter."

"So when will the meeting take place?"

"Tonight. Mr. Zhang insists the meeting take place in his hotel. But I've ensured you will be safe. I have my people in place. You will then pass the original to him, and he will give you the fake. A simple deal, I think you'll agree?"

"More than simple." Lucia narrowed her eyes in thought before facing her mother once more. "Too simple, do you think?"

Her mother's face broke into a slight smile. "You have more of me in you than you believe, my daughter. As soon as you have completed the switch, then my men will reveal themselves and ensure you leave swiftly and go directly to the airport."

"So, I won't see you again before I leave?"

"No. It's better that way."

"Better for whom?"

"For you, of course." She rose. "Now, return to your hotel. I'll make sure you are safe there." She waved a hand and Lee appeared as if from nowhere. He must have heard everything that had been said. "See to it."

"Yes, madam."

She rose and beckoned to Lucia. Although she must have been around fifty years of age, the woman's still-dark hair was worn long and she was dressed in a figure-hugging cheongsam. She reached out and touched Lucia's cheek and, for the first time, Guy saw the woman's composure crack a little.

"I thought I would never see you again."

"But I'm here, now."

"And then you'll be gone. Will you return?"

Lucia smiled briefly. "I will. I can't live in your world, Mother, but I will see you again. And, you know, you can always come to visit me."

"Maybe I will, Luli." She nodded as if giving permission, and Lucia stepped forward and kissed her on both cheeks. Her mother's hand lingered a little on Lucia's shoulder.

As her mother turned, the lights from the crystal chandelier seemed to catch in her eyes, making them glint and sparkle, as if full of tears. She disappeared through doors which opened and closed for her by invisible hands.

They walked out of the building, and Guy looked at the impressive facade. "Your mother is something else."

Lucia smiled. "She certainly is. It was good to see her and know that she loves me and wants us to be reconciled."

"When did she tell you this?"

"Just now."

"But—" Guy had no recollection of any of these words being uttered.

Lucia stopped walking and placed a hand on Guy's arm. "Guy, these things might not have been said. God knows, so little is ever actually said in my family, but it's understood. She used my Chinese name. That says a lot."

"Well, I'm glad you understand because I'm totally out of my depth here. It's all too subtle for me!"

Lucia laughed. "Maybe that's why I like being with you so much. I don't have to try to understand you."

"Yeah, compared to your family, I'm an open book. But tell me, why didn't your mother want to come to the meeting?"

Lucia swung around on her high heels to face him. And he was once again reminded of the incredible likeness to her beautiful mother.

"Guy! My mother doesn't attend meetings. For one thing, it's too dangerous, and for another, she doesn't get involved at the operational level. That's what Lee Kun is for."

Lucia started walking away again and Guy watched her

go, wondering how the hell he'd got himself involved in this strange world, with this woman he thought he knew.

The chimes of a nearby clock struck eleven, its metallic sound barely reaching beyond the hotel building, drowned out by the busy traffic along Shanghai's main street.

"Are you quite sure your mother can protect us?" asked Guy, casting an anxious look down the street. "I hate to bring it up, but she couldn't protect your brother."

"She didn't know how deeply he was involved. She'd deliberately distanced herself from the organization's details. That all changed with his death. Believe me, her influence will protect us."

Lucia cast a worried look at Guy. This wasn't his world —she didn't even want it to be hers anymore. But for tonight, it had to be.

They'd been over and over it because Guy wasn't happy with Lucia taking the lead. She realized it went against everything he believed in, but she hoped she'd finally persuaded him. She also knew that he was concerned about her pregnancy.

It was hot and humid outside. But they were only on the sidewalk for the few seconds it took between leaving the hotel and entering the air-conditioned limo in which Lee sat, as calm as if he were taking them on a sight-seeing tour.

Guy stepped in after Lucia, carrying the bag which held the painting.

Lee nodded when he saw the bag and glanced at his Rolex watch. "We should be there in a few minutes. You've told Guy what will happen, Lucia?"

Guy rolled his eyes and looked out the window at the

beautiful colonial buildings that lined the grand boulevard. Lucia knew his macho pride had been dealt a severe blow by having to play a supporting role.

"Yes, Guy understands what's about to happen," Lucia replied.

Guy sighed. "Yes, Guy knows he's not to say or do anything. Guy knows it's all down to Lucia now."

Lee's lips quirked into a rare smile. "Good."

They turned off the main road and drove into an underground carpark. Lee gave Lucia a reassuring nod. Lee hadn't kept her mother and family safe for so many years without his famed attention to detail. Her mother's people would be there, even if she couldn't spot them.

"Where's the back-up?" Guy whispered to Lucia. "I don't see any."

"If you saw them, then don't you think the owner of the hotel would also notice them?"

"Good point."

Lucia quashed the nerves in her stomach and inhaled the chill air-conditioned air, overlaid with the sweetness of incense, and she channeled her mother. She felt the familiar icy calm come over her. She was glad that Guy seemed to have withdrawn into himself because it made it easier for her to become the woman who was her mother's daughter.

The elevator doors slid open to reveal two guards standing outside a door. One of them opened the door and Lee entered the room and spoke in rapid Mandarin.

Lucia turned to see who he was talking to. There were three men. But it was the man leaning against the ornate mantelpiece to whom Lee spoke. The man was tall for a Chinese man and had the air of a debonair European, complete with beautifully tailored suit and haircut in the latest style. He was also younger than she'd imagined. His eyes were sharp. He wasn't looking at Lee; he was looking at her. Automatically she tilted her chin in defiance. She wouldn't show weakness before this man. She felt Guy also respond to the challenge and come up behind her, his hand on the small of her back. It gave her the confidence she needed.

"Greetings," she said in Mandarin.

"And greetings to you, gracious daughter of a most esteemed lady," he replied in Mandarin. He gave a small smile. "I think we can proceed in English now, for the sake of our Kiwi friend."

Lucia felt Guy tense. He hated being called by the name of a nearly extinct flightless nocturnal bird. "Yes, of course."

"Please be seated."

Lucia would have preferred to stand, but she knew she mustn't do anything that could lead to this man losing more face than he had already. So she sat, poised on the edge of her seat, legs folded under her, in the same manner her mother sat. Guy glanced at her and took his cue, and also sat, for once a reserved look on his face. She gained strength from his confident manner which she knew wasn't feigned. Guy wasn't a man to be frightened of anything. Even though he ought to have been, given the situation.

"Would you care for refreshment?"

"No, thank you."

"Then perhaps we should get down to business."

"Of course."

"You have the painting?"

Guy pulled the painting carefully from the bag. Lucia had taken it out of its frame. Seeing the reverence with which Guy handled his painting did something to Lucia. It was *his*—his family's, depicting one of his ancestors, a New

Zealand icon—and to think they were being held to ransom by this businessman who'd tricked Guy's parents into selling, offended her deeply.

Mr. Zhang nodded to one of his staff who brought out a painting, also out of its frame.

"May I?" asked Lucia, indicating she'd like to inspect it.

He agreed, and she walked over to the painting. It was a brilliant forgery. And she suspected she knew the artist—a New Zealander who'd been arrested on forgery charges some years before. She also knew, without a doubt, that she was the only person in the room, possibly in New Zealand, certainly in China, who would be able to tell the difference between the forgery and the original. The forger had been clever and had used the same canvas and trim on the painting. The two were indistinguishable to the lay person.

She bit her lip as she tried to repress the preposterous plan that had instantly formed in her mind.

"Take the forgery," said Mr. Zhang dismissively. "I have no interest in anything that is not authentic." He pulled the sleeve on his Armani jacket. "And pass the original to my man."

She did as she was told.

Mr. Zhang was so nonchalant that he turned to Guy to speak. It was only then that she realized the man holding the painting was in her mother's employ. It was in his eyes. He lowered his head imperceptibly and glanced away. There was no one looking at her now. She held the original in one hand, and the forgery in the other. She quickly made a decision.

Guy didn't take his eyes off Mr. Zhang. He didn't trust him as far as he could throw him. While Lucia was alone with one of his henchmen, swapping the paintings over, the businessman beckoned Guy over and showed him his other paintings. The man appeared to have originals from every country in the world, locked up tight in this inner sanctum which only a few people could access.

"And you, see, I needed one from New Zealand. Now, I can say I have originals from every civilized country in the world."

Guy grunted, angry at the thought that one of his country's treasures was being bought simply to complete a collection. Why the hell didn't this man take up stamp collecting instead?

"I'm ready," said Lucia. They both turned to her. Guy frowned. For a moment, he thought he saw a spark of something in her eyes which was at odds with the frozen expression of earlier. Then it was gone.

He held out his hand for her and she picked up the forgery and walked toward him, rolling it as she went.

"One moment," the businessman said, tapping out the cigarette on the ashtray. "Let me see."

Lucia turned on her heels and, with a slight smile unraveled the painting before the businessman's nose.

"I can't see so well here. Bring it to the light."

They both went, and after an intense search, the businessman turned to Guy. "Enjoy your forgery, Mr. Martin."

Guy nodded, biting back the bile in his throat. He'd have liked to punch this man's self-satisfied face but knew he wouldn't make it out of that room intact if he did.

"Thank you," he managed to say.

"*Shi péi le,*" said Lucia politely, bowing slightly.

To Guy's surprise, the man bowed back. "Send my regards to your mother."

"I will."

Lee opened the door for them and they walked out into the foyer and straight into the waiting elevator.

Inside, Lucia handed the painting to Guy who stuffed it into the case and lifted Lucia's face to his. "You're pale. Are you okay?"

"I'm fine."

"Are you sure? The doctor said that too much stress might hurt the baby and that was pretty damned stressful in there."

Lucia shot a look at Lee who didn't return her gaze, but simply continued to look straight ahead.

"I'm fine," she said softly to Guy. "Fine."

Smoothly, Lee slipped away, and another man appeared and took them to the car. By the time they were seated, Lee reappeared and slipped into the passenger seat beside the driver.

"Apologies. I was called away. We'll go directly to the airport. Your return flight is ready to take off as soon as you arrive. It seemed prudent given the circumstances."

"Of course," muttered Guy, sweeping his hands through his hair and loosening his tie.

It was late and the traffic, while always bad, had thinned out allowing them to reach the airport without delay. As soon as they left the car, the heavens opened, and they ran across the rain-slicked tarmac to the steps which led to the plane. They bade hasty farewells to Lee and were seated, belted, with the engines roaring into life, when Lucia looked out and saw a figure, standing beneath a large umbrella held by a man. The figure held up a hand to Lucia. Lucia swallowed a lump that had sprung from nowhere. It was her mother. And the man holding the umbrella, in an unusual job for him, was Lee Kun. He'd told her mother that she was pregnant. He must have done.

That's where he'd disappeared to for the minutes it had taken to get into the car. She should have guessed.

Lucia raised a hand to her mother, but it didn't seem enough, that solitary signal. And she pressed her fingers to her lips, kissed them and blew it out to her mother, just as she'd used to do as a child, before she knew that it wasn't the done thing. Of course, her mother had never done that. Never reciprocated and Lucia had learned from her.

But now, Lucia could hardly believe her eyes, as her mother pressed her own fingers to her lips, closed her eyes briefly, and then waved her hand in a gesture both of bene-diction and love.

"Thank God that's over and done with." Guy sighed and sat back in his chair. "How are you? Are you okay?"

"Sure, I'm okay. Why wouldn't I be?"

"No reason," he said, taken aback by her sharp response. What was up with her? She hadn't been the same since they'd left her mother's place. From the moment she'd been with her mother she'd slipped into the ice queen mode. Necessary, he supposed, for what had followed but he'd been waiting for her to relax, to be her real self ever since. And it hadn't happened yet.

He signaled for a drink refill. As the whiskey poured into the glass, he watched her sit totally still as she checked her emails. She didn't even seem to be reading them; she stayed on one for a long time.

"Actually, there is a reason," he said, replacing his drink. "I'm worried about you."

"Worried?"

"Yes, worried. What you did back there was remarkable.

I don't know one woman in a hundred who'd have done that, risked her life for me. But ever since we've been alone, you've made excuses not to talk to me. What's going on, Lucia? Is it the stress of what happened or is there something else going on that I know nothing about?"

She bit her lip and averted her gaze. There *was* something going on. "I think it's all to do with the stress."

He wasn't satisfied with her response. It seemed like she was talking in code. "What is? Have you had a change of heart about our future?"

She placed a hand on his arm. "Please, Guy, can we leave it? It's been a difficult twenty-four hours, and I'm exhausted."

He felt a total bastard. What the hell was he doing? The poor woman was pregnant and drained—no small wonder she wasn't upbeat and chatty. "Hey, I'm sorry, Lucia. The steward said the bed's made up. Why don't you sleep?"

"I don't think I could sleep even if I wanted to. Maybe later. I'll just go to the powder room."

Guy watched Lucia walk to the toilet and wondered if she'd ever return to the way they were. If she'd ever lose that reserve.

Lucia knew what was happening. Even if she hadn't read the books, or heard from her girlfriends, she knew instinctively that she was losing the baby. It hadn't happened yet, but it had begun.

She'd rung her doctor from the plane's bedroom. He'd told her what to expect. Bleeding. But not too much to begin with. That would come later, after they landed in Wellington probably. There was nothing a doctor or hospital could do at this time. The pregnancy was too early, and the baby wouldn't make it. She'd wait it out in the apartment, and then if things didn't resolve themselves easily, she'd make arrangements to go to the hospital.

As she returned to her seat, Guy smiled at her hesitantly as if not knowing the kind of reception he'd receive. And he was right. She couldn't feel natural, not with how her body was fighting her.

She opened a magazine, focusing on calming the tremor in her hand. It worked. She studied the form of the model, so beautiful, so unemotional and wished that it was her. A blank two-dimensional figure in a magazine with no life to hurt her. She glanced at the caption without reading and then turned the page.

She heard Guy sigh beside her as he flicked through the channels on the big screen in front of them. A steward appeared from nowhere with a headset for him and a refill for his drink.

He was drinking too much. She just wished she could. But she felt sick. Part of her wanted to tell Guy what was happening but another was scared, way more scared than she had been in Shanghai. He'd said he wanted a future with her and their child. Would he want a future with only her? Getting pregnant had been a fluke this time round. Chances were, it wouldn't happen again. He'd finally come to terms with his past, and was looking forward to a life that she could no longer give him. Should she wait and watch as he slowly drifted away from her? Or should she finish it now, to save them both from unwanted pain?

CHAPTER TWELVE

It was business as usual in Wellington. Guy could hardly believe it. After all they'd been through together, Lucia had disappeared. He'd last seen her when he'd dropped her off at her apartment, not understanding but respecting, her request to be alone. But she hadn't been there the following day when he'd called. She still responded to his texts, reassuring him that all was well, and that she simply needed to be alone for a few days. But Guy knew something had gone wrong, something major, something which suggested his future was about as rosy as the dim, yellow light emanating from behind the bar he stood propped against.

The nightclub music throbbed from the next room, and Guy ordered another drink. "Dallas?" He held his glass in a query.

"No." Dallas rose from the barstool. "I've had enough club sodas for one night. And you've had more than enough whiskeys."

Guy ignored him, and ordered another one.

Dallas sighed heavily and sat. "If you're going to keep me here all night, then at least talk about Lucia."

Guy grunted and swirled the amber liquid in the cut glass before taking a drink. "No point."

"I think the point is pretty obvious. You're in here, drowning your sorrows and God knows where Lucia is. Something's happened, and I want you to tell me what."

Guy sent daggers at Dallas. "Don't you think I would, if I knew?"

"You've done what I told you not to do, haven't you? You've gone and hurt her."

"Hurt her? I haven't done anything except support her. Well, in recent weeks at least. No, there's only one person who's been hurt around here, and that's me."

It was Dallas's turn to grunt. "Only one person feeling sorry for himself, that's for sure."

Guy glared at Dallas. "She got to me, Dallas, like no one else has."

"Then what the hell are you doing here, gazing into a glass of whiskey, rather than Lucia's beautiful eyes? It was the first thing I noticed about her. That brown, it was like chocolate. Deep."

Guy stilled. He didn't look at Dallas. His mind was fixed on the mental image of Lucia's eyes. Dallas had described them exactly. They weren't only beautiful. They were deep. So soulful, you felt you'd get pulled in and could drown in them.

"She has depths," Dallas continued.

Guy glanced at Dallas, suddenly irritated by the reminder that Dallas and Lucia had dated. "Why you ever finished with her was beyond me, when you like her so much."

"You know why. Because she wants far more than I can give her. What she wants, my friend, is someone exactly like you."

"Yeah, right. If she does, she's not showing it. I think she's changed her mind."

"She has feelings for you—strong feelings—and if you can't see that, then you're a bigger fool than I thought."

"I'd like a chance to see it! How can I when she won't tell me where she is, won't let me see her? I don't know what the hell's going on. And, frankly, I'm concerned. What you don't know, Dallas, is that she's pregnant."

Dallas swore under his breath. "Pregnant? Good God! Unexpected but brilliant news for you both. It's what she's always wanted." Dallas clapped Guy on the back, and Guy nearly choked on his whiskey. Guy rolled his eyes. "So why the hell you think she's having second thoughts is beyond me. Everything is going according to plan."

"Whose plan?" asked Guy.

"Mine, of course."

Guy suddenly felt stone cold sober. Dallas was right. Lucia should be happy, and she wasn't. Something had gone wrong. He pulled out his phone and rang Rachel. What he heard had him jumping up from the stool.

"About bloody time!" said Dallas, shrugging on his suit jacket. "I'll take you home and then you can get round to Lucia when you've sobered up in the morning."

"No. She's in the hospital. Rachel's just left her. Take me there. As fast as you can."

Lucia awoke from the anesthetic not knowing where she was, but knowing that she was no longer pregnant. It had taken a few days between the first indications that not all was well and losing the baby completely. She'd imagined it would happen easily—simply slipping away from her body

—but there was nothing easy about it, and Rachel had taken her to the hospital. Everything had happened swiftly after that.

And now, any remains of her pregnancy had gone, clinically removed, as if it had never been there. She felt a deep void inside—physically and emotionally. She lay looking at the wall, not wanting to turn and face the world.

How was she going to cope with her loss—a loss she feared she'd never be able to replace? She closed her eyes tight against the early morning light which, as soft as it was, was too bright for her eyes which stung from too little sleep, too much time spent staring her bleak childless future in the face. Nurses moved back and forth, their soft-soled shoes squeaking on the polished floors, the trolleys rattling as they began their rounds. Business as usual. But nothing would be the same again for her.

She wouldn't cry anymore. She'd shed enough tears to last her a lifetime. She inhaled slowly, noting the feel of the breath in her throat, in her mouth, drying her already dry lips. This was real. This was life. She had to go on.

She rolled over, opened her eyes, and gasped. Sitting in the chair beside her was Guy, fast asleep, his hand resting on the pillow beside her head, as if he'd fallen asleep with his hand on her head.

Rachel must have told him. She'd asked her not to phone him, but she guessed he must have rung her.

A window was open, and the net curtains flapped lightly in the breeze. The soft gray light caught Guy's cheek, highlighting its sharp plane, and the shadows under his eyes. He looked exhausted. His jacket was slung care-lessly over the chair, and his shirt was open, revealing a chest she'd lain her cheek against in weeks past. She looked at it, and wondered how she'd ever had the confidence to do that—it felt out of reach now.

She felt humiliated by her body, by her inability to keep the one thing she'd always wanted, and the one thing that had made her and Guy believe they had a future together. Her baby had been the glue that had joined them together and given them a joint vision of the future. And without her baby? She didn't know if they had a future.

But he was here, now.

She reached out to touch his cheek, rough with stubble, but stopped before she made contact with it. The urge to feel the reality of him, to take comfort from his presence, was strong. She knew that touching him would take some of the pain away. But what if he didn't want that? What if he was only here because he was doing the right thing by her? What if this was the beginning of the end?

She pulled her hand away. She made no noise but his eyes opened immediately, and he sat forward, his gaze searching her face.

"Lucia! You're awake! How are you?"

"I'm fine." She tried to smile reassuringly, but it wouldn't come and faded on her lips before it had begun. She eased herself up in bed but felt suddenly dizzy. "At least I think I'm fine."

"Don't move. Is there anything you want?"

"Water, please."

He stood, poured her a glass and held it to her lips. She drank quickly as his gaze held hers. He replaced it on the nightstand.

"Better?"

She nodded. "Did Rachel tell you?"

He took her hand in both of his. "Yes. I wish you'd have told me."

"I'm sorry, I didn't know what to do." She shrugged. "I guess I was scared."

He frowned, shook his head and sat back. "You'd have been less scared if I'd have been with you."

She pressed her lips together and was silent. "It was more than the miscarriage; I was scared to have my fears confirmed."

"Tell me," he insisted in a low, firm voice.

She cleared her throat. "I knew how much you wanted the baby. Okay, maybe not at first, but you came to like it. You committed to me purely because I was pregnant." She ignored his shake of the head. He was decent, kind and wouldn't want her to believe that, even if it were true. "I didn't tell you because our whole future was based on having the baby. And without the baby..." She let the unspoken words hang between them.

"You thought I'd leave you."

She nodded, only just managing to suppress a sob. "It crossed my mind."

"Why? Because you truly believe that I'm the kind of man who'll leave the woman he's going to marry if she suffers a miscarriage?"

"Marry?"

"Yes, Lucia Rossi, I'm asking you to marry me."

"Why?"

"*You*, Lucia Rossi, must be the most distrustful person I know. I want to marry you for the usual reasons. I love you. *You*. Yes, I wanted the baby and the vision of a future for us all, together. But none of it would have meaning without you. I don't *want* any children if I can't have you. I don't *want* anyone but you. No one. Nothing. Just you. Get it, Lucia? I only want *you*. No one else. No conditions. Just *you*. Have I said it enough times to convince you? Lucia, you stubborn woman, will you marry me?"

She tried to hold back the tears.

His eyes narrowed. "No, I was wrong. There is a condition."

"What?" she whispered.

"You have to be more open with me. You have to trust me from now on. Okay?" He caressed her cheek.

"I will," she said.

He held her face between his palms. "You'll always tell me what you think?"

She nodded. "Promise. Beginning now. I love you, Guy. And I want to marry you and spend the rest of my life with you—with or without children."

He held her steady gaze. "At last, we've found something we have in common. It might only be one thing, but it's pretty damn big, and pretty damn real."

The beginnings of her smile melted away as he pressed his lips to hers, sealing the promise with a kiss.

Guy listened to his parents but was only aware of Lucia by his side. He held her hand tightly in his. He'd made sure he rarely left her side over the weeks since her miscarriage. He needed her to know he'd always be there for her.

She glanced at him with a smile.

"Come with me, Guy," said his father. "I want you to go over these new plans of yours for the estate."

Guy rose, and he and his father walked away talking about the developments Guy had in mind for the vineyard on the Onihau Estate.

Guy looked up from the papers his father was showing

him and watched Lucia. It was his new hobby, watching her. He particularly liked to do it when she wasn't aware of being watched. Only then could he easily read her. Like now, instead of walking across the sitting room with her usual graceful steps, she hesitated by the Goldie painting. She cocked her head to one side and narrowed her eyes. Then, very gently and with infinite care, she adjusted the painting, before standing back to admire it. Then she smiled, and carried on walking.

Guy frowned and looked at the papers. But he wasn't listening to his father. He remembered the first time Lucia came to Onihau and the way she'd straightened the Goldie. He frowned. *She couldn't have.* He looked at her and she smiled as if she hadn't a care in the world.

"Lucia?" Lucia turned to see Guy's mother, Barbara, beckon her over. She joined Barbara across the other side of the room. "Have you heard from your mother recently?"

"Yes, frequently. I've told her everything, and she's even saying she may come to visit next year."

"Good. I'm glad. We can't begin to repay her for all her help over the painting."

"I never did understand why the men who bought the painting from you believed they had the original."

"Hm." Barbara glanced across at the two men who were deep in conversation, looking over plans. "Well, I guess I *may* know."

"Really?"

"I'd always loved that painting, and the thought of it hanging in a dusty museum—the thought of her, Guy's great-great grandmother—hanging in a dusty museum, it didn't seem right. She's family, you know? I didn't want her in an institution." She paused, smoothed out her dress. "I'd hoped it wouldn't go ahead, but then the two men—supposedly from the museum—turned up one day with the painting, the forgery, and the cash and offered a swap there and then." She glanced at her husband who was still talking to Guy. "Don is a very pragmatic man. He didn't want the worry of looking after a valuable work of art. He's not interested in art, not like me." Barbara shrugged. "He also likes to talk and show off Onihau, so he took the men off to look around the estate, leaving me with the two paintings. They were identical. If I hadn't known where the original was placed, I wouldn't have been able to tell them apart."

Lucia followed Barbara's gaze to the Goldie, now hanging in the large reception room.

Barbara turned to Lucia with a smile. "Would you like some more tea?"

"No!" Lucia took a deep breath. "Please, carry on with your story."

Barbara shrugged. "Not much more to tell really. The forgery, as I say, was very good and I knew none of the men could tell them apart. But I could. Simply because I'd been there the whole time." There was another pause as they both looked toward the Goldie once more. "Things can get switched around sometimes. I did love the original so."

Lucia burst into laughter, and Guy and his father turned around. Guy smiled to see Lucia laughing. Lucia looked at Barbara who was watching her closely.

"I think you like the real thing, too," Barbara said.

The laughter subsided, and Lucia nodded. "And I've found it... in Guy."

EPILOGUE

A freezing mist hung over the rugby pitch. The mountain range behind them was iced with snow. Lucia shivered and pulled down the hand-knitted beanie which Hannah's grandmother had knitted for her. Hannah's family had welcomed her into their extended family with open arms. She waved to one of them on the opposite side of the pitch. She'd be catching up with them all later.

She watched as Guy kicked the ball up the pitch and went hurtling after it. He, and the others in the team, came charging down the field toward her. People all around cheered, and she suddenly thought maybe she should too.

"Go, Guy!!" Lucia called out from the sidelines as a rugby player slid by on the soggy pitch, showering her with thick, sticky lumps of mud. "Ugh." She grimaced as she felt a hand on her arm and Dallas pulled her back. "You're over the line, sweetheart." He grinned at her as she sheepishly took her place beside him and his two brothers, Callum and James.

"Sure," she said, embarrassed. She was way out of her

comfort zone here but she was beyond caring. Since she and Guy had become engaged, every day was different; every day was an adventure.

Dallas and Callum watched the game, muttering things to each other, while James paid more interest to a beautiful blonde who walked by. The whistle blew, and Lucia realized she'd forgotten to watch the game.

"Is it over?"

"Yes."

"Who won?"

"Guy's team."

Together they walked slowly back to the club rooms where Guy would join them after he'd showered.

James had hooked up with the blonde and appeared to be making swift headway. Callum was talking farming with Guy's neighbor, and Dallas was checking stocks and shares on his phone. Three powerful, sexy men. Three powerful, sexy bachelors. Lucia couldn't help wondering what kind of women they'd end up with, whether they'd find anyone who'd be strong enough to match their own strength, anyone who could deal with the baggage they carried.

Lucia shrugged. Who knew? It would be interesting to watch, though, she thought to herself.

Guy came up behind her, put his arms around her waist, and pulled her to him.

"Ogling the Mackenzie brothers, my love?"

She twisted around in her arms. "Never. I'll leave them to some poor, unsuspecting women. I've enough on my hands with you."

He grunted softly, and his hands dipped a shade too low down her back, as his fingers swept the top of her bottom. "Sure do. We've our baby to make."

She bit her lip. "But what if we can't? It's been months now and nothing."

He brushed her lips with his. "It doesn't matter. I love you. All I want is to make love to you... baby or no baby."

She sighed. Who could argue with that?

———

AFTERWORD

Miscarriages are heartbreaking and I used my own experience when describing Lucia's reactions. Luckily for me, just over a year after my miscarriage, I gave birth to my beautiful daughter. But Lucia's physical problems are more complex and the chances of her conceiving, more remote. But I promise, you *do* learn what happens to her in later books in the Mackenzies series :)

In the meantime, Lucia is very happy. She's finally found her home—with Guy, his family, and their friends, the Mackenzies. Often in our complicated lives—where we are separated from family—our friends step in and become part of our family. And having family—blood relatives or friends—is so important to our happiness.

And family is what the Mackenzies series is all about. The series continues with *Secrets at Parata Bay* which tells the story of Dallas, Lucia's ex-boyfriend. He's a powerful, uncompromising man, and he falls for a woman with a secret. The road to their happiness isn't an easy one...

The setting for Parata Bay is, in fact, at the end of the road where I live. Apart from doing away with the neighbors, the view is just as I describe it in the book. It looks out to an island and has a sweeping bay at the bottom of the cliff. I've lived here for over twenty years and it's a very special place —not least because it's home. And we all need one of those don't we?

Sophie

SECRETS AT PARATA BAY

BOOK 2 OF THE MACKENZIES—DALLAS

SOPHIE HAYDON

A grieving mother intent on revenge. A million-aire who values honesty above all else. A love threatened by the legacy of family....

Cassandra Lee is a woman on a mission. She's lost both her son and father in tragic circumstances and she's determined to exact revenge on the man she holds responsible by attacking the only thing that matters to him—his wealth.

And Dallas Mackenzie's wealth is important to him. He's spent years intent on two things—being the opposite of his father and restoring his family's fortunes. But, in so doing, he's created an emotionally empty life for himself.

But empty lives can be filled—at least for a short while—and Dallas sets out to seduce Cassandra. Unfortunately neither seduction nor falling in love with this powerful man were things for which Cassandra could prepare. She just hopes that his interest—and her resistance—will hold out long enough to ruin him...

Excerpt

The restaurant had once been a private villa. Prestigiously perched on the hills overlooking Wellington's glittering harbor, the grand old house now catered for patrons who desired privacy and were used to the best. And Dallas often enjoyed the discretion it offered. Never more so than now, as he sat back and watched Cassandra order her dinner from the waiter.

She was an enigma and it only intrigued him more.

The usual response to an apology—especially by a new employee—would have been either a polite rejection of its necessity, or a polite acceptance. Which meant Cassandra was neither acquiescent nor polite. Despite a slightly ruffled ego, he liked that.

He also liked the way her straight, dark hair shone in the candlelight, revealing subtle highlights that couldn't be reproduced in a hair salon. The depth of color provided a stunning foil to her pale skin and deep blue eyes. Irish coloring, he guessed. Wherever her family originated from, she was very beautiful.

He took a sip of soda water and placed it carefully back onto the table between them, as he tried to control his visceral reaction to her. He looked up and caught her gaze. He realized his attempt at control had failed; he was incredibly attracted to her. Years ago, he would simply have taken her back to his apartment and they would have made love all night. But he had the feeling one night wouldn't be enough.

His errant thoughts of how much fun pleasuring this woman would be, were interrupted by the waiter bringing the drinks and responding to Cassandra's enquiry about the restaurant's history.

Dallas only half listened as his eyes wandered back to Cassandra. Her chin was tilted up as she looked at the waiter, revealing her long neck which, God help him, he had an irrational desire to lick. Her hair fell, straight as a die, down her ramrod straight back. There was a slight stiffness to her elegance as if she were conscious of every movement, not entirely at ease. When the waiter left and she turned back to catch his gaze, he could see the unease in her eyes too. She was holding something back, but he'd find out what it was. Later.

Find out more!

ABOUT THE AUTHOR

Hello!

My name is Sophie Haydon and I write romances with stories which make you turn the pages, and characters who feel real.

I'm an avid people watcher, hopeless romantic and dreamer who spends far too much time gazing out the window, imagining scenes where people struggle with life and emotions but always end up happily. Because, yes, I'm also an eternal optimist!

I currently have two connected series — Mackenzies and Lantern Bay — which feature the Mackenzie and Connelly families. All the books I've written so far are set in New

Zealand, where I live. But I was born on the north Norfolk coast of England and am planning a series set in the small seaside town in which I grew up. And then there's my Nantucket trilogy which I began planning years ago, but have yet to find time to write.

So, wherever you are in the world, welcome to my little corner, where I sit with my two cocker spaniels snoring gently beside me, creating worlds where people struggle with life and emotions but are always rewarded with love and happiness in the end. Because that's non negotiable!

I hope you enjoy my books.

Sophie

x